The problem of the weight of African-American public opinion had been the subject of several meetings between Malan and several prominent American politicians.

"You've got to understand, Colonel, these people have the vote. They carry political weight. We're definitely in your corner all the way but we have to tread lightly at this time."

"Senator, I can only say to you one thing, the loss of South Africa to the communists would be disastrous to your country's economy."

"I can assure you that many of us realize that, Colonel."

The idea of using drugs against an enemy did not disturb him at all. Everything was fair in war.

He slid back underneath the covers, feeling sure, powerful. Yes, drugs would do it. Why spend ten million developing a program that only offered a fifty percent chance of success? When the drugs guaranteed success.

He slowly sat up in bed and wrapped his arms around his knees.

The South African economy would be bolstered a thousand times. Gold, diamonds, uranium, cocaine.

The irony of it almost caused him to laugh aloud.

What greater revenge could one achieve? Selling to the enemy and destroying him at the same time.

CONSPIRACY

ODIE HAWKINS

Originally published by Holloway House Publishing Company

Copyright © 1993, 2012 by Odie Hawkins

Front cover photo by Zola Salena-Hawkins,
www.flickr.com/photos/32886903@N02

ISBN: 978-1-5040-3584-2

Distributed in 2016 by Open Road Distribution
180 Maiden Lane
New York, NY 10038
www.openroadmedia.com

CONSPIRACY

Prologue

After tripping halfway around the world he finally decided to pay us a visit in Atlanta. Muntuna and the children went damned near out of their minds with excitement.

If I had been a jealous type, I would've been walking around with my jaws tight every day, just from checking out the attention my wife and children paid him.

"Herb, Leon says I shouldn't let the children eat candy, or any of the stuff that has refined sugar in it, just fruit."

"Dad, Uncle Leon is teaching me Capoeira Angola, it's more ritualized and more serious than Capoeira Regional."

"Daddy, I love Uncle Leon, he's so funny."

Well, that gives you some basic idea of the family vibe. And to tell the truth, I was right in there with the rest of 'em, tryin' my level best to make sure that his six-month stay with us was going to be one of the best times he'd ever had in his life.

He showed up looking lean, fit, and full of fun. Nothing like what I expected after reading his last three books.

"Herb, you've got to remember something, man: a writer is a lot like an actor. If a writer tried to seriously feel all of the emotions his craft required of him, he'd be stark ravin' crazy in a week. I can write about bitterness, but I'm not bitter. I refuse to be bitter. I can write about sadness, but I ain't sad. I can express a lot of feelings but they're not necessarily how I want to live my life."

I don't know if they arranged it that way, but Simone, the librarian that he had given his soul to, down the road a ways in Augusta, was spending time with her youngest daughter up in Alaska.

Muntuna kept up with everybody's business. "I don't know, baby, what do you think? You think she made it her business to get outta town 'cause she knew Leon was coming?"

"How did she know he was coming?"

"Well, I had to tell Lucille, and once you tell Lucille anything, you may as well say you've told Augusta."

"I'll have to remember that."

He was family from Day One. And he still had a bunch of strange ideas about a lot of things. I challenged him on one of his pet theories.

"How're you going to prove what you're saying about the Afrikaner-dope connection?"

"I'll write a novel about it."

"But Leon," I argued with him over a fifth of Chivas Regal, "that wouldn't be considered proof of anything, that would just be another novel."

"You may be right, man, you may be right, but I'm gonna write the motherfucker anyway because I believe it could've been true, or it might've been true. Here, hook me again."

He started on this thing the next morning. I could see the

8

change come over him. He was still Leon on leave, having a good time in Georgia, but a focused look had come to his eyes. And he was doing some slightly different things.

"Damn, Leon, you're doing an awful lot of runnin'; man, you training for the Olympics?"

"Nawww, I'm just taking a week to shape up for this book."

It didn't take a lot of reasoning to figure out why the dude was in such good condition. If he started training like that before every book...

I got in the habit of jogging again and lost ten pounds in three days; running in that Georgia heat can melt your ass.

Next thing he did was go to the library. Muntuna cracked up, "He ain't likely to find Simone down at our local library, is he?"

He got down to business exactly one month after his arrival, I clocked him. What is it that them white boys used to say on the west coast? "It was awesome."

He wrote in the morning, before we got up, wrote a little in the afternoon, and then far into the night.

I'd never spent much time around so-called creative people. He acted like somebody who was "possessed." Muntuna worried about him.

"Herb, did you notice him making notes or something while we were having dinner?"

"He's always making notes, or something."

Two months later he eased up and began to talk a li'l bit about what was happening with him.

"Herb, you've really got a beautiful family, man, beautiful. If anybody had ever told me that I'd be able to write in a household with four teenagers, I'd've called them liars.

"I appreciate the non-interference while I was struggling to get the powder burns on the paper."

"I don't know if I clearly understand..."

"Well, I don't know how it is with other writers, but for me I need to jump in there at the beginning and get that nut, you know? That takes the edge off. After I get that nut, I can sorta settle back and do some after strokin'."

"You make it sound like a love scene."

"For me it is. I can get into foreplay for years, and sometimes it'll take a while for that orgasm to come through, but after that everything is jelly-jelly."

He spent a couple more months rewriting sections of "A Conspiracy."

"Why are you rewriting?"

"I'm trying to smooth some shit out, I see some seams showing through, I don't like that."

Three weeks later, after he'd gotten the thing typed and copied a couple times, he put a copy in my hands and said, "Here, man, read this and tell me what you think."

The manuscript that you're about to read is what he gave me to read. He made only one qualification...

"This thing might need a sequel, depending..."

Chapter 1

He alternately slept and gazed out of the window. There was so little to do on a plane. One could stroll the aisles, strike up nebulous conversations with fellow passengers, fix the earphones in place, watch the movie.

Henrik Malan did not care for any of those pastimes, he preferred sleeping and gazing out at the clouds. These two activities gave him the opportunity to rest and focus on the problems he would be forced to deal with when he finally reached his destination.

"Can I get you something, sir?"

"No, no thank you, I'm quite comfortable."

He stared into the stewardess' eyes. A dark-brown-skinned Black woman with blue contact lenses. It was obvious that she liked him. She had shown every sign of being attracted to him after the flight was less than two hours old.

A Black woman with blue eyes, as blue as his own eyes.

11

He decided not to try to figure out why she was wearing blue contact lenses.

He had learned, over the course of many trips to the United States, not to judge the behavior of the African-Americans by his own standards. They were an unpredictable bunch, the American Blacks, a perfect illustration, in his mind, of what happened when inferior people were granted a piece of a superior process.

"Well, if you need anything, just buzz. O.K.?" And she winked.

"Yes, of course."

He smiled at her back as she strutted toward the cockpit.

Women. Women were a species apart, he felt; scrape the skin off of them and no matter whether they were Black, brown, white or any other shade, they still had the markings of a different species.

Why was she attracted to him? Was it because he was "handsome?" He never thought of himself in matinee idol terms. His own reasoning told him that he was a youthful-looking fifty-year-old man, blonde hair streaked with gray, clean shaven, what some people called a distinguished-looking chap, lean and fit from regular exercise and no overindulgence in alcohol and the wrong foods.

He absently fingered the crescent-shaped scar at the right corner of his mouth.

I wonder what she would feel for me if she knew I was a South African, an Afrikaner, a Boer, a colonel in the South African Secret Police.

He smiled again, a wistful smile; who knows? Being a woman, she might find me even more attractive. I would have an "evil" quality that seems to be attractive to some women.

He flashed back to the white American college woman he had met three years before, on a mission to New York.

12

"Are you really from South Africa?" she had asked, puzzled by his slight accent.

"Yes, I am a South African."

He was feeling congenial and felt no need to avoid the inevitable debate he knew that they would have to have. And they had had it.

They continued the debate well into the night, at his hotel, after a good French dinner, wine and cognac. He felt better with a false name, distant.

"Are you actually saying, bottom line, that Black people are not qualified to govern themselves?"

"No, I am not saying that. I'm saying that they are not qualified to govern us."

He had watched her, pretending to be asleep, the following morning, as she scribbled a heartfelt note and tiptoed out of his life.

"Dear John," he nodded off, remembering the contents of the note...

"Dear John, I had to leave before you woke up; I just couldn't bear the thought of being with you any longer. Somehow you don't really seem to be what you seem to be. I hate racism and racists, especially intelligent racists. I had a lovely time.

Sincerely yours,

Mary Beth Sawyer"

How many Mary Beth Sawyers had he been forced to deal with in the United States? He mentally counted three. No, five.

Strangely, he had found several other women who took a position to the right of him.

"I think what you guys are doing is right on. That's one of the problems we've had here because we didn't try to keep our niggers in their place."

Racists. He hated them. He felt that there was something

13

inherently warped about feeling that one race was superior to another.

He had tried to explain his position to an American businessman, on his previous trip to California.

"You must understand, my friend, we are not trying to keep the African in bondage. We are trying to maintain a civilization that he would destroy, if given the chance."

"Say whatever you want to, pal. All I can say to you is this—keep those monkeys under your thumb by any means necessary or else you're gonna have the kind of problems we have here."

Once again, a wistful smile developed. The Americans were so unsophisticated about racial matters. It seemed to be quite simplistic for them: either you kept the Africans under your thumb or you released them.

He made a subconscious groan, and peered down into the sulfite-flaked clouds of the Los Angeles basin.

"Please, adjust your seat belts. We'll be landing at Los Angeles International Airport shortly. Thank you for flying..."

He stared at the city welling up on his right; rows of pillboxes, kidney-shaped swimming pools, monotony. She strutted through the aisle one last time, making certain that everyone had his/her seat belt in place, leaned over to place a slip of paper with her name and telephone number on it in his lap.

Once again he was in Los Angeles, one of the cities in the world he really enjoyed, an insane place, laced with freeways and shopping malls.

He could never put his finger on what he liked about the place. There were several things: the "spread-out flavor" appealed to him, the sense of being anonymous, it was as though you were in a kind of fairyland. And the fact that he didn't feel repressed to the wall by Africans.

"Call me," she whispered as he left the plane, and winked again, her blue contacts giving her a weird look.

He smiled and nodded yes and immediately thought, call you what?

He had five days to do his work, no time to "call" anyone, indulge in sex-fantasy games.

Van Damm was there, almost the caricature of a subservient chauffeur. Malan made a mental note to request that the Consulate get rid of Van Damm, he always greeted his arrival as though he were a Mafia chief or some kind of royal figure. It focused too much attention on him.

"Good afternoon, sir, I trust you had a good flight."

"Good enough."

He handed him the ticket for his bags and, in the process, rolled the stewardess' number into a small ball and flicked it away from him.

He settled into the passenger's seat, feeling slightly rusty from the hours of sitting down, but focused.

"Van Damm, I want you to drive east to Western Avenue, make a left turn going north on Western, and then turn left, going west on Wilshire Boulevard when you get there."

"Yessir."

He felt in tune with a city when he was driven through it, absorbed a sense of its rhythm.

Los Angeles was always changing, in small ways; a new gas station here, a one-story building torn down on this corner, a two-story building replacing it, a small shopping mall overwhelmed by a larger shopping mall, affluence everywhere, even in the Black areas.

He stared at the Black faces as they drove north on Western Avenue. It could be a section of Soweto, he thought, as they paused for the light at Manchester and Western.

"Ever seen so many filthy kaffirs in your life, sir?"

"They are not 'filthy kaffirs', Van Damm. They are

15

underprivileged African-American citizens.''

"Yessir.''

He hated that, the automatic assumption prevalent amongst a certain level of South Africans (and a number of others) that being a South African white automatically translated-equated to being a racist. He freshened the mental notation to have Van Damm fired.

Western Avenue seemed to reveal one of the classical circumstances of America: the familiar stranger-neighborhood.

Now Black, now Latino, now Korean. Korean. He took in the shop fronts, the exotic block lettering. Koreans.

There seemed to be thousands more than he remembered seeing during his last visit.

"Wilshire Boulevard, sir.''

He sighed and settled back. Nothing ethnic about the core of Wilshire, it was a street that was created for money. It could've been one of the main boulevards in Jo'burg.

"I was instructed to remind you, sir, that your meeting with Dr. Allen is for 10:00 a.m.''

"Thank you, Van Damm, I have the schedule.''

The Beverly Wilshire, the top-hatted Black doorman in the black green monkey suit.

"Evening . . .''

He felt bored to the bone after a half hour in his suite. Same old, dreary stuff on the television, same old, uninteresting hotel room. He decided to rent a car. He knew where to go and what to do on a Monday night in Los Angeles.

"This is 515, I'd like to have a car for the evening.''

"Immediately, sir, thank you.''

Fifteen minutes later he was in a rent-a-car, heading toward the Crenshaw Strip.

Wonder if I'll run into the blue-eyed woman in the Pied Piper? Hardly likely, she'd be more likely to be found in the beachfront joints.

He never felt hesitant to tour the jazz points in Los Angeles, the Black good-time spots. Whenever his presence was noted, there seemed to be an immediate assumption, after his "English" accent was noted, that he was an adventurous type who had strayed from the beaten path, along with a few others.

He made an impulsive left turn on Martin Luther King Drive, to Marla's Memory Lane Supper Club.

The odors, the perfumes greeted his entrance. He always liked that. No matter where he went, he knew that he would be pleasantly assaulted by the Black scent.

Blacks, all over the world, he reflected, seemed to love incense, perfumes, pleasant smells. He occupied a seat at the bar and looked the situation over.

It was a bit early, 9:00 p.m., too early for the kind of feeling he knew would develop later.

"What'll you have?"

"Uhh, let's make that a gin 'n tonic."

The men to the left and right of him seemed to relax. He was obviously a foreigner, someone they didn't share mutually bad feelings with. He felt the tension disappear.

Wonder what they would feel if they knew I was Colonel Henrik Malan of the South African Secret Police? He played with the thought for a moment, sipping his drink.

There was a strong possibility that they would ignore any announcement that he was a South African, a "beast" from the "terrorist state." Or maybe they would follow him outside and beat him to death.

He looked around at the audience. A few white couples, one table populated by a mixed bunch, himself, the only single white man in the place.

They must think I'm a "John," out looking for dark meat. Once again he reflected on the dilemma that the African-

American presented. It seemed to be almost impossible to tell anything about their character. They could give the appearance of being calm, easy going, at peace, and then riot.

He didn't feel ill at ease, but at the same time he didn't feel that he *knew* them.

"Uhh, bartender, I'll have another one of these."

He felt the man's peripheral glance.

"You from England?" he asked.

Why not be from England?

"Uhh, yes, how did you guess?"

"Well, I could tell from your accent, but aside from that, I could tell from the cut of your clothes. The English put together some nice pieces."

"Have you been to England?"

"'Bout two years ago, me 'n my ol' lady. We decided to trip out to Europe and we wanted to go somewhere where they spoke English."

"How did you like it?"

"We had a ball."

They were interrupted by the star of the evening . . .

"Ladies and gentlemen, the lady you've all been waiting to see and hear, without further ado, we proudly present the one 'n only Zena McNeil. Let's put our hands together and give her a big round of applause!"

Malan was struck by the beauty of the woman who glided into the spotlight. In South Africa, she would've been classified a "colored," as would half of the Black people in the club, including the man who had opened a conversation with him.

Here, in America, in Marla's Memory Lane, she was simply an African-American singer. And an excellent one.

Once again he was stunned by the immediacy of the feelings that erupted during the set. He had witnessed the same emotions in clubs in Soweto, where his appearance had produced a much more subdued effect.

The club was bubbling after the singer's appearance.

"Lady's too much, ain't she?"

Too much? It was not a Pidgin, it really was another language.

"Yes, I guess one could say that."

It was time to go, the animation produced by the singer and the effect of three gin 'n tonics warned him that it was time to go, time to get ready for tomorrow.

"Check, bartender."

"You leavin', man, it ain't really started happenin' yet."

"Gotta go, busy day, lots to do, you know how it is when you have a few days and lots to do."

"Hey, I can dig where you comin' from."

He stared at the man's outstretched hand for a moment. Blacks were so...so innocent...so quick to grant their approval. He shook the man's hand.

"Give my regards to the Queen. Name's Jessie."

"By all means, the minute I see her, Jessie."

"What's your name?"

"Paul Marley," he answered, without thinking about it.

"You any kin to Bob Marley?" the man asked, with a broad smile.

"No telling, Jessie, the Marley tree had a lot of branches."
The man smiled and waved to him, full of goodwill, as he made his way away and out of the bar.

He drove supercautiously back to his hotel. They'd made a big deal of any South African being cited for anything on the streets of South Central Los Angeles after dark.

South Central Los Angeles. He dismissed the familiar, sinister sound of it as he looked through his messages.

"Dear Col. Malan, welcome to Los Angeles...." Stupid Vervoerd. He had no sense of secrecy. Anything that happened was worth a telegram, purely for the sake of form.

Did it ever occur to him that he might not want certain people to know he was there?

The rest of the messages were like junk mail. If anyone was listening, they'd have to believe that a member of the South African Secret Police was in town. He shook his head in disbelief. It was incredible about the "American" operatives; after a year they became so "Americanized," they needed to be replaced.

He gazed out at a full moon before nodding off. Jonas Vervoerd offered his usual nervous greeting. "Welcome to Los Angeles, Colonel Malan."

"I received your telegram, Vervoerd," he said dryly and seated himself behind the bureaucrat's desk.

"Uhh, yes, of course."

They stared at each other for an awkward moment, Vervoerd wringing and washing his hands as usual. It was always difficult to have members of the Secret Police visit the Consulate, they seemed so cold and rigid.

"Dr. Allen will be arriving shortly. In the meanwhile, I have several suggestions to make. Number one, I would prefer that Van Damm not be employed by us any longer. You may give him two weeks' severance pay."

"Van Damm? He's one of our best..."

Malan stabbed the nervous bureaucrat with a cold glance.

"Yes, of course, we'll see to it immediately."

He made a mental note to have Vervoerd replaced. America seemed to cause a terminal weakness of some sort, he noticed. After a couple years some people had to be replaced because they had become soft, or weakened in some way.

The secretary's voice spilled from the intercom.

"Dr. Allen is here, sir."

"Thank you, allow me five minutes and then send him in."

"Yessir."

20

"Vervoerd, you have an option, you can be a part of this meeting or not."

"If it's just the same with you, Colonel Malan..."

"I am simply Henrik Malan here, how many times do I have to remind you?"

"Uhhh, sorry sir. If it's just the same with you, I have other matters to attend to."

"Suit yourself. Send Dr. Allen in, please."

Yes, there was definitely a need to send men like Jonas Vervoerd back home periodically, to "stiffen their backbones."

"Good morning, Dr. Allen, welcome to a bit of South Africa in America."

"Good morning, Mr. Malan."

"Please be seated."

Henrik Malan made a quick reading of Dr. Marcus Allen, again. Definitely an academic, but there was nothing of the absentminded professor about his manner. It was quite easy to see, behind the black horn rims, a sharp mixture of cynicism and intelligence.

Dr. Allen was one of the principal architects of his country's television image. He was the one who had warned them to take the heroic images of young Africans off of television.

"Don't you see what's happening? Even apathetic types are beginning to relate to their struggle—you must remove those images from the tube if your government wants to accomplish its aims without outside meddling."

He was a valuable consultant. His fee was large but he was worth it.

"Well now, what do you have for us this time, Dr. Allen?"

He watched Dr. Allen snap his briefcase open and dip inside for a sheaf of papers and a manila folder. "Per your instructions, or should I say, as a result of our last meeting,"

21

a quick, crafty smile, "I've developed four programs, designed for the American market. Each of them has a well-structured subliminal message. I think you'll appreciate the subtle messages contained in each of them."

"Both the president and I have been quite satisfied with your work."

"Thank you. In addition to the programs, I've designed one special, specifically aimed at the Black American audience."

Malan made a mental note of a few key words. He said "designed," not created. "Developed," "structured."

Why was Allen on their side, working for them? The money was obviously an incentive. They had compiled a complete dossier on him: a nagging wife, two children, the girl with a drug problem, an Asian mistress, flying trips to Las Vegas. But there was something else.

He never felt completely at ease with Allen's lack of scruples. He seemed to be willing to do anything, for a price. And there was a danger in that. If he were willing to create/design programs for them, was he just as willing to do the same for others?

"The Black American special will focus on an African hero, someone they can relate to and yet be distant enough from him not to cause any...problems."

"What's the payoff for my government?"

"As I see it, the payoff will be political, initially, but I have no doubt that making an effort to influence Black Americans will inevitably result in financial gains.

"Blacks will spend their money freely, with only the slightest encouragement."

"Even with us?"

"I'm sure a few well-designed, mislabeled corporations could correct that problem."

Malan folded his hands on the desk top and glanced at the

stand-up calendar in the right corner—It's Sunny Today in South Africa.

"How much will all of this cost?"

Dr. Allen pushed his glasses up onto the bridge of his aquiline nose and studied a sheet. "I think the total package would be assembled for...ohh, about ten mil or less."

"Hmmmm...that doesn't seem to be an unreasonable price to pay for goodwill."

Dr. Allen beamed, he could already see the smile on Sumiko's face. She loved him more when he was successful.

"However, I don't think it's quite what we want at this point in time."

A vicious little smile played at the corners of his mouth, watching Allen's glasses slide down, the gleam dying in his eyes.

"I have a feeling that things have gone too far for us to make a hit with TV specials, no matter how cleverly they are designed and structured. We need something else, something heavier, that will have a greater impact."

"What...uhh...what do you have in mind?"

"We thought you'd be able to come up with something."

"I would be willing to stake my reputation on the possibility of the..."

"Let me speak frankly, Dr. Allen. You have made several worthwhile contributions to my country's welfare. I just don't think this is one of them. I have a gut feeling that making an effort to expose an African hero on American TV might be counterproductive for us.

"We need to have negative exposure of Blacks whenever possible, not positive. Negative. Do I make myself clear?"

Dr. Allen nodded solemnly, avoiding the direct gleam of the laser-beamed blue eyes behind the desk. They didn't call him "Iceberg" for fun.

"I don't want you to misunderstand me, Dr. Allen, the

23

use of television is always a tricky business. It may very well be that your programs would have the desired impact, but not for long. That is one of the great problems in that area, whether pro or con, the effect wears off too soon. We want a carefully designed program that will have a lasting negative effect.''

"I understand, Mr. Malan. It appears that I'll have to return to the drawing board.''

Dr. Allen returned his sheaf of papers and manila folder to his briefcase. They stood and shook hands.

"Mr. Vervoerd will, of course, negotiate a suitable fee for your time and an option on the ideas that you've designed.''

"Thank you.''

"We'll be in touch.''

He sprawled in his seat and placed his heels on the desk.

This was not the time for pictures that might or might not work, they were at war, and in order for his country to win or at least come through it, they needed something bigger, dirtier.

He mentally reviewed the one major contribution Dr. Marcus Allen had made to his country's media welfare—"You must remove those images from the tube if your government wants to accomplish its aims without outside meddling.''

And they had done that, reduced visual media coverage to file footage. But they had not replaced those images with anything as strong, as pro-government as possible.

As Colonel Henrik "Iceberg" Malan of the Secret Police ("dirty tricks public relations section"), he felt frustrated at not being able to come up with the right formula.

They needed something that depended on a third wheel, in a manner of speaking. Something that would not be so obvious that it was noticeable and yet would have the proper impact.

It's sunny today in South Africa.

"May I come in, Colonel...uhhh, sir?"

"Yes, Vervoerd, come in, the meeting is over."

"Yes, of course. Dr. Allen submitted this account for his services. It seems..."

"Pay him whatever he asks."

"Yes, of course, sir."

"I'm going for a walk. If there are any messages for me, you can have them delivered to the hotel."

He had remembered to bring a pair of sunglasses, an accessory that he had found extremely useful during all-night interrogation sessions.

Beverly Hills, Wilshire Boulevard, at midday.

He strolled east for a couple blocks, impressed but unawed by the giant buildings, a tribute to high finance.

Beverly Hills, Wilshire Boulevard. It could be any large, financially structured boulevard in Johannesburg. He took careful note of the beautiful women and handsome men. He could tell that rugby was not a popular sport from the number of unbroken noses he saw.

Why the hell are we supporting this damned Babylon? he asked himself, walking back to his hotel.

The damned hypocrites confirm every stupid reading that had ever been made of them. They spent thousands of dollars to publish lies and accepted millions in hypocrite money, obviously pleased with the profit margin.

He paused for a bit to eat in one of the swank dining "spas" that dotted the area.

Horrible food, pretentious atmosphere complete with two "stars" that he vaguely recognized from popular TV programs.

Fifty dollars for a piece of stale fish and a dab of some kind of sauce. He felt a real twinge for Cape Natal Lobster and the simple tart sauce that went with it.

The wine was even worse, a complex California vintage that had been frozen to tastelessness.

"Will there be anything else?"

"Do you think I can stand anymore?"

"Beg pardon, sir?"

"Forget it. Check, please."

Beverly Hills was such a cold fish. But so was white Jo'burg, and white London and white Paris and white Lagos. And all of the places that prided themselves on their "whiteness." The racist code designated "white" areas by a money standard. He understood that. But he couldn't understand the rationale that operated as an effort to prove that buying things represented the apex of what was gently termed "the good life."

He paused to window shop a block from his hotel, his mind settling back to the problem of p.r.

The situation was never declared serious, but at the same time all the perceptive members of his government realized that they were in a life or death situation.

Too bad Allen couldn't've come up with something foolproof.

***

He threw himself across his bed, relieved to be out of the sun, away from the false images.

False images: Dr. Marcus Allen, Beverly Hills, Marla's, no, not Marla's. Marla's was "for real." He smiled at his use of what he assumed was a Black idiom.

Marla's. He made a mental note to go back.

He had discovered the African good time style in the shebeens of Soweto, as an arrogant young white policeman.

The more he thought about it, the more he felt that the

26

solution for his problem rested in the ghetto, the Afro-American Bantustan.

They had the raison d'etre for their destruction, he could feel it in his bones.

"This is room 515, I'd like to have a car for the evening."

"What time, sir?"

"Ten p.m."

"Very good, sir, it will be arranged."

A plan was beginning to form in his mind as he showered and shaved. Why not use the same people who were causing so many problems as a diversion, a way to misdirect?

He made a right turn on Martin Luther King Drive, to the Flying Foxx.

They gave him the kind of sophisticated, Black, peripheral attention he had come to expect. A white guy in an overwhelmingly Black bar in the Crenshaw area. He could just as well have been a Korean, for all they cared.

"Gin 'n tonic, please. Beefeater gin."

"You got it."

It wasn't Marla's, there was no act about to go on, no whites but himself. He studied the situation carefully, obliquely.

"How's everything, you got what you need?"

The voice was well modulated, seductive.

"Beg your pardon."

Was the man a pimp? A phony ring salesman?

"I don't know, what do you think I should have?"

He stared at the small glassine packet the man palmed out under the bar face.

"How much?" he asked innocently, fully knowing that he was about to be taken.

"Well, ordinarily, this would be a twenty-five dollar bag but I'll let you have it for twenty."

He spooled a twenty off a slim roll of bills, palmed his

purchase and watched the crack peddler slither away.

Crack, cocaine, rock.

He took a sip of his drink and strolled to the men's room, to get rid of the evidence, vaguely puzzled about his reasons for buying the drug.

He stared at the glassine packet for a moment and suddenly felt the light go on in his head, the flicker that had prevented him from wandering into political ambushes, the intuitive spark that kept him at least ten steps ahead of his colleagues.

Dope. That was the angle....

He watched the packet get sucked down into the toilet.

What was it his mother used to say?

"Henrik, there is a reason for everything."

Dope. Drugs. Crack.

He strolled back to his seat at the bar, nodding a thanks to the bartender for covering his drink with a napkin.

He decided not to finish it off. He had been away too long, someone may have dropped something in it.

He had the angle he needed now, time to return to the real world. He dropped a five dollar bill on the bar and started out.

The pusher made a sly move past him at the door and whispered, "Name is 'Dap Sugar Charlie,' c'mon back through when you need something."

"How do you know I'm not a cop?"

"I know cops when I see 'em, you ain't no cop."

The "Iceberg" exchanged a frosted smile with Dap Sugar, two bastards from different sides of the tracks.

Chapter 2

He slitted his eyes open quickly, disturbed by the dream, laced his hands behind his head and stared at the ceiling.

What had disturbed him most was the crudeness of the "interrogation activity." No, damn it! It had been a torture session, and not a very successful one.

"We're going to make you talk, you damned bloody kaffir bastard! Or else you'll never be able to speak to anyone else again."

He had watched the "activity" from a distant corner, sipping tea. It was obvious that they were not going to make the man give up anything other than his "name, rank and serial number."

They had torn his large toenails out. They had electrified his testicles, smothered him in a plastic bag, made him eat the hair shaven from his face.

His name was Sizwe Makebane. He had been caught red-handed placing a land mine on a white rail passage and they wanted to know the names of the other members of his cell, his collaborators.

"Tell us their names, you black bastard! Or we'll destroy you!"

Malan frowned at the memory of the angry young lieutenant, his fists bruised and bloody from punching the young African in the mouth.

"Lieutenant, may I have a word with you, please?" The lieutenant's expression changed from a worried frown to outright astonishment as Colonel Henrik "Iceberg" Malan gently, but firmly, lectured him on the necessity of being "objective" in his interrogation.

"You chaps are taking this far too personally; let's skip the 'bloody kaffir' business and do the job. That man in there is doing his job. He is refusing to give you information. You are calling him names but not getting any information.

"I suspect that he is gaining strength from your name calling."

"Gaining strength, sir?"

"Yes, I would say that your curses, your emotional outbursts, are causing him to take heart."

"I don't quite understand, sir."

"Makebane is a Zulu, Lieutenant, he is a member of one of the most militaristic tribes ever developed in this part of Africa. You're familiar with Shaka, are you not?"

"Shaka? I'm afraid not, sir."

"Well, Shaka was...never mind. We'll get into that at another time. What I'm saying to you is this: each time you call him a name, you are psychologically granting him the status of a warrior who is being spoken to. Someone who is worth wasting curses on. I daresay, looking at the physical damage that's been done to him, that you would've gotten everything you wanted from him if you had been silent from

30

the beginning.

"These people are vocal types, Lieutenant. Remember that. They went to war chanting in the old days and when they defy us today, they do it by singing. Remember that. They draw strength from noise."

"Yessir, I will remember, sir."

Sizwe Makebane was murdered and the names of his collaborators went to the grave with him.

Malan subconsciously nodded his head in disbelief. The younger people coming along were so, so racist.

The familiar, twisted smile played in the corners of his mouth. The irony of it. The American college girl had called him a racist.

But not the kind of racist who knew nothing about the peoples they had conquered and were losing control of.

He sat up on the side of the bed. They *were* losing control, there was no doubt about it. The core was becoming soft. Hundreds, thousands were leaving.

In the old days the Rhodesians, the Portuguese from Mozambique, all the rest had flooded in, and now they were the first to leave again. They, according to some opinions, knew what a sinking ship felt like.

He walked to the window. Beverly Hills at 11:30, it could've been the backside of the moon. He planted himself in a parade review stance, his right fist cocked on his hip.

Let them all leave. The Afrikaner was there when they got there and we'll be there when they've gone.

He gritted his teeth, filled with a gush of racial pride.

He didn't often allow himself to become flushed with patriotic feelings. He felt that there was a danger of losing a certain sense of balance when one was unbalanced by overwhelming emotions.

One thing is certain, I think we have the solution to one of our most annoying problems. If we can neutralize,

31

demoralize the African-American, we can remove a big thorn from our side.

The problem of the weight of African-American public opinion had been the subject of several meetings between Malan and several prominent American politicians.

"You've got to understand, Colonel, these people have the vote. They carry political weight. We're definitely in your corner all the way but we have to tread lightly at this time."

"Senator, I can only say to you one thing, the loss of South Africa to the communists would be disastrous to your country's economy."

"I can assure you that many of us realize that, Colonel."

The idea of using drugs against an enemy did not disturb him at all. Everything was fair in war.

He slid back underneath the covers, feeling sure, powerful. Yes, drugs would do it. Why spend ten million developing a program that only offered a fifty percent chance of success? When the drugs guaranteed success.

He slowly sat up in bed and wrapped his arms around his knees.

The South African economy would be bolstered a thousand times. Gold, diamonds, uranium, cocaine.

The irony of it almost caused him to laugh aloud.

What greater revenge could one achieve? Selling to the enemy and destroying him at the same time.

He drifted off to sleep with the name of the Black dope dealer on his mind...Dap Sugar Charlie.

The morning meeting was scheduled for ten o'clock, as usual, with his counterpart in the C.I.A.

He had already decided to cancel any other business he might have in the U.S. His decision was made and he knew what he had to do.

"Mr. Smith is here to see you, sir."

"Send him in, please."

He shot Vervoerd a malevolent look, to tell him to get a grip on himself, to stop fidgeting. Yes, Vervoerd was definitely in need of a "back stiffening."

"Mr. George Smith," M.A. from Yale, Ph.D. in philosophy from the University of Chicago, C.I.A., ruthless, a brother.

"Good morning, Mr. Malan, Mr. Vervoerd."

"'Morning, Mr. Smith."

"Smith" smiled pleasantly at the two South Africans and settled himself into the chair in front of Vervoerd's desk, the seat behind it occupied by Colonel Henrik Malan.

"Well now, it's been a while since we've had a little chat, hasn't it?"

"Yes, it has been a while."

The two men allowed a comfortable pause to settle between them.

"So, what brings you to Southern California?"

"Shall I say . . . recent events in Southern Africa?"

"Smith" edged forward slightly, the traditional chit chat cut to the marrow.

"And what has been happening in Southern Africa that we should be informed about?"

"The heads of two major front-line states recently had a meeting."

"Smith" cocked his salt-and-pepper-streaked head to one side, curiously.

"The meeting concerned the possibility of using nuclear weapons in their struggle against my government. Were you aware?"

It was impossible to tell when "Smith" was surprised. Or lying. In this instance, he looked surprised, but it could've been an act to cover up his lie.

"We knew about the meeting. As a matter of fact, we had a couple of our people there, taking notes, you might say."

They exchanged spy-smiles, leaving Vervoerd to cope with the gray areas.

"But there was no record made of the nuclear capability."

"That item on the agenda was not listed. Which one of them has it? And are you certain?"

Malan named the country, feeling fairly certain that they already knew. The C.I.A. was not likely to be caught unawares by any African nation in possession of nuclear arms.

"Are you planning a preemptive strike?" Once again he felt at ease about making a reply. They obviously had the answer to that question or else he would never have asked. It was an old game that lawyers all over the world played. Never ask a question unless you have an inside track on what the answer was going to be.

"We haven't considered that as a priority at this point."

"What conditions would determine your priority?"

"It would be difficult to say at this moment. However, we think that we can neutralize the situation by creating incompatible circumstances between the two allies. We happen to know something about the chinks in their particular armor."

"Well, as you know, we owe you guys a big favor."

"We intend to call upon you at the proper moment. Can we offer you tea?"

"I'm afraid not, I have to get back to a pile of papers on my desk."

"I quite understand."

"Mr. Vervoerd, Mr. Malan, a pleasant day to you both."

They exchanged pleasant nods as he exited.

"Very interesting man, 'Mr. Smith', isn't he?"

Malan tented his hands under his chin, thinking, already beyond the important codes that they had exchanged.

"Yes, he is," he answered Vervoerd's question without

34

considering the source.

He liked "Mr. Smith," the ruthless quality of the man. He knew enough about his background to know that the man was equal to ordering a murder. Or committing one. It was documented in his life.

He wrote, erased, rewrote and restructured ideas in his head as the plane droned back to Africa. It was a talent he had developed as a defense mechanism after a scrap of paper he had made notes on had been reproduced a hundred times by a mean-spirited superior, years ago.

"Does everyone have a copy of Lieutenant Malan's important note?"

He winced at the memory. No notes. Keep it all in your head.

In his head he was evaluating the best approaches to make to the president. He's such a stiff-necked old Boer, a Laager mentality if ever there was one.

He felt certain that he would have no trouble convincing their leader that a few more members of the ANC should be assassinated, but to convince him that they should sell drugs, even to their enemies, was going to take careful positioning.

As usual, he was surrounding himself with all of the support material/possibilities necessary. He tossed the alternatives up in the air and juggled them from one side of his brain to another.

He knew he could depend on his contacts in the Israeli Mafia to supply them with all of the cocaine they needed. They would, of course, attach riders to the agreement but they would work that out.

He had already decided, in addition, to make use of his connections in Argentina. The unreconstructed Nazis living there would jump at the opportunity to saturate the ghettos.

So, the Blacks think they have a drug problem now. They

35

ain't seen nothin' yet!

***

He paid close attention to the president's eyes as he came to the conclusion of his presentation. His eyes became veiled, almost sleepy, looking behind his glasses when he was deeply interested in a subject, wide open and glazed when he was bored. Or in total disagreement with something.

Malan was pleased with his work, the president looked sleepy.

"Whether we like it or not, Mr. President, these people represent a veritable powerhouse of public opinion. If we can neutralize, destabilize this element, by the means that I've suggested, we can be absolutely certain that many of our American friends will return.

"I can assure you that they have only placed a slight distance between us in deference to public opinion. I think this is also the case with others who do not feel at ease, frankly speaking, about the situation we find ourselves playing on the world stage, especially in our region."

"What guarantees can you offer that the drug plague you intend releasing on the American Bantustans will be contained?"

"I think, sir, without exaggeration, that the American police departments have an excellent record of keeping the hard drug problems within certain boundaries. We can, of course, secure greater cooperation by including a select number of our more sympathetic friends in this enterprise."

"We won't be able to do that, Henrik, we must go it alone. No one must know that the 'cocainization' of the Bantustans is a part of our disinformation policy. Are we clear on that, Henrik?"

"Uhh, yessir."

36

The president stood, the caricature of a beer-bellied burgomeister, but there was nothing fat about his brain.

He walked around the polished oak table, smiling, and clapped a ham-like hand on Henrik Malan's shoulder.

"You've done excellent work, Henrik. Excellent work. I would suggest that you take a few days off, do a little fishing down at the Cape."

"The idea appeals to me, sir, but I must begin to develop my team, work a few kinks out."

"Yes, I understand. It sounds like exciting work. Two years, you say?"

"We should begin to see tangible evidence, businesses attempting to sneak back in within a year. The actual profits from this operation should accrue within a few months or less."

"The cocaine trade is that lucrative, eh?"

"Yessir, preliminary research indicates an overwhelming profit margin in the trade."

He was tempted to say, "Dap Sugar Charlie told me . . ."

"Well, good results and fine profits never offended any God-fearing Afrikaner. Your budget is unlimited, subject only to my disapproval. Once again, congratulations."

He shook the big man's fleshy hand, feeling somewhat humbled by the man's grandness. He was called Oom ("Uncle") and it went well with his personality.

"Oh, sir, there's one thing more."

"Yes, what is it, Henrik?"

"I think Vervoerd should be replaced. He seems to be a bit shaky."

"I've already seen to it, I could feel the shakiness happening in Pretoria."

"Thank you, sir."

"If there is anything else you need, you know the number to call."

"Thank you, good night, sir."

Malan marched downstairs to his office, feeling exhilarated. He was being given a fair chance to turn American (and world) public opinion around slightly, maybe more than slightly.

The TV screens would be flooded with drug-crazed gang members lined up against walls, not children fighting tanks with stones.

He had divided the United States into four regions: The California Region (from California to Colorado). The Middlewestern region (from the Mississippi River to Virginia). The Plains Region. The Eastern Region (the east coast down to Florida).

He kicked his heels up on his desk.

Cocaine, one of the most addictive drugs ever discovered was now going to become one of South Africa's most valuable allies. The white powder comes to the white man's aid.

There was a good deal of pre-operational research to be done, the delicate problem of selecting regional coordinators budgets to be designed. But the important thing was in motion, the die had been cast, they were in business.

He had one more important consideration to make, whether or not he was going to deal with the Israeli Mafia or the "Argentineans," the old guard Nazis in that country.

The irony of being forced to think of two such groups caused his twisted smile to develop. Israelis or Nazis.

"I'll deal with both of them."

The telephone ringing disturbed him, so few people had his office number.

"Yes?"

"Henrik, please don't hang up!"

He had to smile. How could she have gotten his number? She must have a secret service of her own.

"I have no intention of hanging up. How did you get this number?"

"It's a long story, one that I don't want to tell you in any case."

"So be it. Well, what can I do for you, Greta?" He felt her indignation swell and burst into the telephone, once again.

"What can you do for me?! What can you do?! Henrik! I am your wife! Have you forgotten?!"

"You are my wife in name only and don't forget it. You are also the wife who committed adultery on numerous occasions with the colored man who used to be our butler. What was his name, I can't seem to recall?"

"Henrik, how can you be so cruel? That was five years ago. Won't you ever forgive me?"

"No."

"Can you swear before God that you've never committed adultery, that you've never sinned?"

"I've never been caught."

The familiar sound of her crying disgusted him. Why did she always have to end her conversations with him in tears?

"Henrik, what are you doing to me?! I no longer have any friends, no one to talk to. All I can do is sit here. You make me feel like someone who is banned. Is that it, Henrik, have you instituted a ban on me?"

"Greta, I have no idea what you're talking about."

"Yes, you do, you know you do. You have isolated me so completely that I feel like I'm dying, right here in the middle of this city. Why don't you give me a divorce, at least?"

"Divorces do not look good on official records."

"What should I do, Henrik?! What should I do?!"

"You have two choices...."

"Yes?"

"Leave the country or commit suicide."

39

The steady flush of tears became a series of broken sobs.

"My God! You are so cold, like a snake."

"Good night, Greta."

He hung up and made a mental note to have his number changed again. Stupid, neurotic woman, she never understood, cannot understand that we are at war with an enemy who could crush them with the sheer weight of numbers, if they lowered their guard an inch. And she had "submitted" to one of them.

Again, he flirted with the idea of having his wife, the beautiful, auburn-haired Greta Berglauche, declared a colored person and divorcing her on the grounds that she had misrepresented her ancestry before they married. He decided against it because of the negative effect it might reflect on his judgment.

No, better to let her rot in her own juices.

He returned to the problem of assembling four regional coordinators, men and women who understood the American psyche and would ruthlessly follow his orders.

Each of the four could pick up a couple local people to actually do the dirty work, but would have to be completely responsible for the operations carried on in their regions.

The names flashed through his mind like cards on a Rolodex.

John Van Niekerk, the California Regional Coordinator.

Hans Botha, the Middlewestern Regional Coordinator.

Anna Viloen, the Plains Regional Coordinator.

Claus Van Der Merwe, the Eastern Regional Coordinator.

The team was there, waiting to be assembled. Now, the most important thing.

"This is Colonel Malan, I want to have flight connections made for Haifa, Israel, on Friday."

"Yessir."

He sprawled back in his seat with his hands laced behind

his head, feeling pleased with himself.

Joseph Levi, alias Joseph Bar-Yehuda, a.k.a "Jo-Jo" and "Haifa Joe," was his primary contact man for anything that needed transshipping, whether legal or illegal.

"You want this? How many? When? You want drugs? What kind? When? From where?"

"Haifa Joe" had, at one point, become the unofficial source for amphetamines in Southern Africa. They felt it was necessary to pep up their "labor units," so they had made a deal for millions of Dexedrine pills and other types of "uppers" to be sold in the labor hostels and townships.

A senior member of the Ministry of Native Affairs once joked at a meeting that "South Africa has the thinnest, fastest moving labor force on the continent."

After "Haifa Joe," Strausser in Argentina. He knew with Joe it would only be a business deal. For Strausser, it would become a crusade.

"Cocaine for the schwarzes? Ja, gut! Ja, gut!"

Chapter 3

He stood with his hands clasped behind his back, allowing the full measure of his presence to take effect.

He was Colonel Henrik Malan and they were his agents. He chose to be slow, deliberate. There were no "presidential sleepy eyes" at this meeting.

"I have chosen the four of you for a special assignment." He paused to give impact to his speech.

"If anyone has the slightest doubt that you will be unable to give this assignment your complete devotion, I ask you to leave the room at this time."

He made a glacial study of each of their faces. He took note of the fact that Hans Botha swallowed hard.

"Good. I knew that I had made the right choices."

He gave them the bare bones of his plan and then, once again, offered the option for anyone to leave if they wanted to.

Professionals, they knew at this point that they would not be allowed to live because of the information they'd been exposed to. He was pleased to note that Botha was smiling.

"Each of you will be given all of the help necessary to infiltrate the communities that you will become a part of. Our American friends have assured us of their complete cooperation, as long as there is no publicity concerning their participation in this operation."

He had played a cat 'n mouse game with "Mr. Smith" before disclosing a substantial portion of his plan. "Mr. Smith" was honestly impressed.

"I think it'll work, Mr. Malan, I really do. Incidentally, we've conducted a high-level surveillance of the suspected nuclear power and I'm pleased to say it was just simply a lot of hot air being blown out."

He wanted to inform "Mr. Smith" that they had checked the matter out weeks before.

"Good, I'm glad to hear that. We might've had real difficulties if they had nuclear capabilities."

He ended his briefing with a customary, "Questions, anyone?"

The quartet exchanged glances, their faces glowing from the anticipation of being allowed to participate in such an exciting operation.

"If there are no questions at this time, you are dismissed. You will be involved in an intensive 90-day training cycle, to familiarize you with the product you will be dealing with, the areas of distribution, African-American history, behavior and matters of that sort, which will begin tomorrow morning. I thank you for participating in this activity."

He stopped Hans Botha as they filed out.

"Botha, you are uneasy about this operation in any shape, form or fashion?"

"No sir, I am not," he answered and met Malan's level

gaze evenly.

"Good, just thought I'd ask."

Joseph Levi, "Haifa Joe," saw it as a unique business opportunity.

"But let me ask you this, Mr. Malan, how do you plan to protect your turf? I don't know if you're aware of it but there is a great deal of competition already in that market."

"I'm aware of that, Mr. Levi. We have no intention of staking a claim to any 'turf'. We simply want to saturate the existing 'turfs'. We know that you and your associates can help us accomplish this. We have no intention of personally fighting with the gang-distributors in any of the major population centers. We simply want to conduct a successful public relations campaign."

The man they called Haifa Joe laughed for a long time. It was so funny to him.

Malan hated Joe. He hated the man's lack of integrity, his lack of ethics.

He had questioned him once about his criminal activities in Israel, a Jew in Israel.

"I am the same as you are in your country, Mr. Malan. It means nothing to me to be a Jew, an Israeli. I am simply a man with an ambition to become extraordinarily rich and, God willing, I shall."

The two-day visit with Karl Strausser in La Rioja, Argentina, had been a much more pleasant one.

"I'm seventy-eight now, Henrik, and there are not many of us left but we have prospered."

They talked about the hellish days at the end of WWII when it seemed that they would all wind up at Nuremberg.

"We will always be grateful to South Africa for offering us a helping hand when we needed it."

It was after a lavish Bavarian dinner, with brandy and Cuban cigars on the veranda of Herr Strausser's finca.

"Herr Strausser, I'm here to ask your cooperation in a great new venture that my government, my agency, is undertaking."

The old man turned to him with a sly look in his eye after he had explained how badly they needed his connections to funnel cocaine into the Bantustans of the United States.

"Henrik, your timing is exquisite. One of the sons of a dead comrade, God bless his soul, a scientist, has created a synthetic cocaine."

They stared into each other's eyes for a long moment, the implications of the discovery obvious to both.

"Synthetic cocaine?"

"Yes. Being a scientist means that he must test and retest to be absolutely certain. But he is ninety-eight percent certain at this time that his product is a perfect imitation of the real thing. He seems to have only one concern."

"And what is that, Herr Strausser?"

"That the synthetic product is twice as addictive as the real item."

They toasted each other's health with one-hundred-year-old brandy.

"I would be honored to meet the scientist."

"I've invited him and a number of other comrades for lunch tomorrow, to welcome you."

"Your hospitality is unequalled, Herr Strausser."

Henrik Malan read until one in the morning, too excited to sleep. What great luck! Synthetic cocaine. It would prevent him from ever being concerned about supplies being cut off from Columbia, Bolivia or Peru. The men and women who milled about the estate grounds the next day could've stepped from a picture postcard of Bavaria. Or Pretoria. Half of the men were past middle age but they were well balanced by a younger group, people in their thirties and forties.

"We've done well here, Henrik. There is not one drop

45

of alien blood in the bunch. As you can see."

"How did you do it, if I may ask?"

"Imports, my friend, well screened imports, mostly from Bavaria."

Karl Strausser marched from one clot of guests to another, exchanging bawdy jokes, tickling apple-cheeked Munchkins under their chins, enjoying an occasional stein of beer.

"Henrik, this is the young man I spoke to you about, Dr. Sigfried Kaltenbrunner, Herr Henrik Malan."

They bowed slightly to each other as they shook hands.

"I am very pleased to meet you, Dr. Kaltenbrunner."

"And I to meet you, sir, Herr Strausser has always spoken well of you."

Once again they exchanged slight bows.

"Gentlemen," Karl Strausser whispered through his walrus moustache, "I think that you might enjoy the privacy of my library. Sigfried, you know where it is. I will have one of the servants bring you a couple cognacs."

"Thank you, Herr Strausser."

He nodded to people he had been introduced to, following the scientist into the mansion. It was a replica of many of the great houses he had visited in his own country, the only difference was that the servants here had brown skin and straight hair.

A servant trailed them with glasses and a bottle of excellent cognac. They settled themselves on a sofa, surrounded by many of the books that Adolph Hitler had burned in his surge to power.

"Dr. Kaltenbrunner, I'll come right to the point: my government is in need of the product that you have synthesized. We are willing to offer you a realistic price for the rights to the formula or for regular shipments of the product."

Dr. Kaltenbrunner gazed around the room, seeming to

study the titles of a few of the books.

"I spent many hours in this library when I was younger, cramming my brain full of facts, figures, and, at times, pure philosophy. The philosophy usually came from discussion between my father and Herr Strausser. The topic of their talks was usually of the New Third Reich."

Malan studied him closely.

"I don't think that anyone has any illusions about establishing a New Reich anymore, but there are still things to be done in the name of Adolph Hitler."

Malan took note of the gleam in the scientist's eyes.

"No, we may not be able to establish a New Third Reich but we can do a great deal to make this world a better place for people of our blood to live in. I will help your cause in every way possible."

They gently clinked their cognac glasses together.

"To Adolph Hitler."

"To Adolph Hitler."

He really meant it when he said, "I regret having to leave so soon, Herr Strausser, I wish I could stay longer."

"You are always welcome, Henrik, always."

Dr. Sigfried Kaltenbrunner decided that he would keep his formula but he would personally oversee the establishment of a factory within South Africa's borders. Henrik Malan, seeking to prevent any trace of a connection to his country, made a decision to set up the factory in one of their Bantustans.

From one Bantustan to another Bantustan was the private joke he told himself.

The machinery was oiled, the people being trained, pre-operational procedures ironed out. He felt a bit strained.

Maybe the president is right, a little vacation might be in order. He decided to charter a fishing vessel at the Cape and pretend to do some fishing.

Henrik Malan, of the Malans of Pretoria, loved his country, the vast open places, the plateaus and mountains. The vivid colors that swept past his eyes.

The colors of his country's people constituted a special treat, even the Africans. He always felt a certain delight in shocking his more conservative colleagues by reciting history and facts about the Black population.

"Of course they were here when we landed, man. This is Africa, the original home of Man, of the African. It's idiocy to say that they weren't here because they didn't greet our ships when we came ashore.

"Africa is African and we took it from them, exactly the way our brothers took America from the Indians."

"If you believe that, Henrik, then how the hell can you support apartheid?"

"Apartheid, my friend, has nothing to do whatsoever with who was here first, it has to do with separate development. And, as we all know, nothing ever develops equally, not even twins.

"The great mistake the African has made is to involve himself in our politics. He wasn't cut out for the viciousness of the European political systems. And his leaders have done him immeasurable harm by pushing him into these systems.

"If we can knock Mandella and the ANC out and a few of these other radical organizations, the African will be much better off. Many of the sensible ones already recognize this and give us all the assistance that they possibly can."

***

John Van Niekerk took his notes in shorthand, determined to record all of the instructor's words.

"The American Black was a much less docile animal than our native variety. He had been thoughtlessly pumped full of white genes and ideas that caused him to be basically neurotic. This neurosis was most evident in ghettos.

"These were confused people who asked for economic and social equality but seemed to reject it if it were offered on white terms. Obviously a contradiction.

"The Blacks were prone to alcoholism, drugs and immoral behavior."

He made a marginal note: "Sounds like Soweto, or Crossroads."

"The so-called war between Black men and women was to be exploited by any means possible.

"Black men, especially the upper middle class types, were addicted to European women. They sought to excuse their addiction by suggesting that it was their way of 'getting back' at their former masters. In some cases, this is true.

"Special note: Black women (of all colors) are extremely sensitive, could be valuable sources of information and comfort."

(Comfort? What did that mean?)

"Be extremely careful of Black men who wear hats indoors, they are known to be notoriously anti-white.

"American whites, in general, were prone to be apathetic about what was happening in the ghettos, but one had to be careful because there were always a few crazed liberals who were willing to start trouble.

"The worst type of Africans had been enslaved and transported to the Americas, the scum of Africa, and, after a period of benevolent slavery, grouped themselves into ghettos.

"So-called African-American history was largely designed to soothe the outraged consciences of small groups of Anglo-Americans who had fallen into the exotic racial trap.

"African-Americans were, as a group, quite happy and pleased with the status quo. Newspaper headlines, to the

49

contrary, were largely the creation of a small, but well organized, group of Jewish anarchists.

"Americans of all colors disliked Blacks because they were considered criminally inclined."

John Van Niekerk, the future cocaine gauleiter of California, reviewed his notes. He had lived in America, briefly, over the course of the past five years, and felt on top of things. He felt that there were areas in which his instructor could've used some instruction, but he felt no need to push the issue. He was being granted the assignment of a lifetime and felt no compulsion to "rock the boat" even slightly.

Colonel Malan, the arrogant bastard, was a genius. There was no doubt in his mind that Colonel Henrik "Iceberg" Malan was the asshole of the century, but the p.r. genius that South Africa had been waiting for, thirsting for, was on the scene.

He felt blessed to have been chosen to be one of the Four, an obscure lieutenant in the Interrogation Bureau (torture squad).

The advice that Malan had once given him echoed in his consciousness, "They draw strength from noise, remember that."

He had validated that on his assignment trips to America. There was no need to be clandestine in America, things were so open that the most secret things could be discussed. It was most un-South African.

"Well, John, you've been to America. What do you think of the lectures?"

"I think that a small percentage of the information that we're being given could use some revision."

"What percentage, would you say?" He knew, because they had all been trained in the same module, that she was going to report their conversation.

"Ohhh, I'd say...one percent, at least."

She bared a crocodile smile at him and marched away to her quarters.

She was going to have tough times in America, he thought, even with the whites. It was difficult to explain, even to himself, why he felt specifically a negative vibe about Anna Viloen. One of the problems he knew she would face when she got to America was her lack of a sense of humor.

Anna Viloen, a solid Teutonic type if ever there was one. He felt certain that she was going to be a disaster area amongst the Blacks, but there was no guarantee. The instructor, as misinformed as he was about certain areas of African-American feeling, was certainly on the money when he stated, "American Blacks, seemingly like Blacks around the world, are totally eclectic. They can absorb attitudes, ideas, religions, philosophies, senses of aesthetics, people, as easily as...as...the Swiss...hahhahhahh....

"We cannot offer you at this time any sensible rationale for this ability to gobble up alien qualities and maintain their own sense of being. All we can say is this, is that the bastardization of their race has created a unique ability to absorb free-flowing attitudes. Brazil and the United States are laboratories of this attitude."

Anna Viloen was too severe, too ordered. He sifted her region through his head; the Middlewestern Region—that took in Chicago. She was in for trouble. She'd be lucky to survive a year with that bunch.

He felt extremely fortunate for having been selected for California. California was the sun, sea, mountainside views, unusual behavior in expensive restaurants. He had to admit, to himself, that none of his experiences in California had taken in "The Black Experience."

During the course of the time he had spent there, he had not had any relations with Blacks. South Africa offered him

51

more of an opportunity to interface with Blacks.

In America, living in Santa Monica, he had attended classes with Blacks, watched them, compared them to the Zulus and Xhosas that he knew (as servants) but had avoided getting to know them. Who wanted to have anything to do with Blacks unless you had to?

He studied his notes carefully. The colonel was right, even if they did not possess the capacity to govern, they were still worth studying, to determine their survival techniques, like roaches.

Anna Viloen sat at her writing desk, the jet-black hair that was usually curled into a bun at the back of her neck flowing down her back in shimmering waves.

"Mr. John Niekerk expresses great doubt concerning Dr. Shagger's lecture on the African-American. He has indicated, on at least three occasions, his disagreement with many of the points that Dr. Shagger has made.

"It must be said, with complete candor, that Mr. Niekerk's remarks were not made to reflect discredit on the professor's lectures, but rather as an indication that he knew more about some areas than the professor.

"I have no doubt that Mr. Niekerk is a very intelligent person, and will do an excellent job with his assignment, but I must admit to a few reservations concerning his personality.

"He seems to be a bit too full of himself at times, unnecessarily cocky, arrogant.

"I hope this report will not be misconstrued as a matter of personality differences, or personalities clashing, but rather as an objective assessment of a fellow coordinator."

She read the note aloud, to get an idea of how it might sound to Colonel Malan. He had encouraged them/ordered them, during private sessions, to make reports on their fellow coordinators.

"I'm not going to ask you to go against the grain, or to act as a stool pigeon. But I do want your honest opinion, each week, of your fellow coordinators. It is extremely important that we should not send one weak link to America. Are we clear on that? Each week."

Van Niekerk wandered around the grounds of the estate that they were being quartered in, trained, wishing he had a cigarette.

No smoking was the rule, a glass of wine with dinner, and when they were not in class, hours of physical exercise.

"You will be subjected to enormous stresses and we all know that the healthier a person is, the greater stress he or she can cope with."

Van Niekerk looked up at Anna Viloen's window and thought, "The bitch! She's probably writing a hate report on me right now."

He had developed a style of reporting that limited his remarks to two paragraphs of general information about each coordinator, including Anna Viloen.

"Hans Botha, the Plains Regional Coordinator, offers us a deceptive intelligence. He does not seem to be as sharp, mentally, as he really is.

"I think this deceptive quality will stand well for him. We are not often blessed with qualities that directly aid us, they usually have to be cultivated."

Chapter 4

Claus Van Der Merwe, Eastern Regional Coordinator, is almost an ideal choice for his post. He gives the impression of being an aggressive Jewish cab driver in New York.

If he has one quality that needs polishing, in my opinion, it is his tendency to be lecherous. I have observed him looking rather closely at Anna Viloen's legs, buttocks and breasts.

***

Anna Viloen, Middlewest Regional Coordinator, needs to "loosen up" a bit. She gives me the impression of someone who could benefit from several glasses of cognac at one time.

She is, in my opinion, an attractive woman who could utilize her attractiveness to a greater extent.

***

Colonel Malan studied the reports, reading between the lines, evaluating.

An excellent quartet. He felt as though he had assembled a quartet of string players, a chamber group, that he could play like a puppeteer.

They would be "graduating" in another month, ready and anxious to work for their country's welfare.

He mentally clicked off the list of things that had been done and those things that were yet to be done.

"Haifa Joe" had, for his usual high price, channeled pounds of cocaine from his South American contacts into the four regions they had targeted. It was waiting for the distributor schedule.

The regional coordinators were being given the best environments for them to deal from that gold, diamonds and uranium could buy.

Each of them was being set up in a style that would allow them to live affluent lives without attracting attention.

John Van Niekerk, playboy-art gallery owner. "I think if I should happen to meet any of the people I know, they wouldn't be very surprised at my occupation. They always thought I was a kind of crazy Dutchman, anyway."

Hans Botha, real estate agency owner.

Claus Van Der Merwe, stock broker. "Let's pray that the market doesn't take a dive while I'm there."

And Anna Viloen, the owner of "Viloen's, a Jewelry Store for the Discriminating Person."

The president had expressed some concern about the two drug sources.

"I don't quite know if I understand this, Henrik. You have paid this Haifa person a sizable amount of government money for shipments of this drug. And, at the same time, you are telling me that Dr. Kaltenbrunner is manufacturing a synthetic version of the stuff in Transkei. Why pay for the real thing when you can get more of the synthetic for less?''

''You have a perfect right to be puzzled, sir, please let me explain.''

The president's eyes narrowed to slits as he slumped to one side of his chair and propped his chin on his palm, his listening posture.

''We have made four initial purchases from 'Haifa Joe', Joseph Levi. This is to bring us into the market place.

''We are now finished with Mr. Levi, he has served his purpose. We were able to take advantage of his 'import system' in order to have stocks on hand when our coordinators arrive. Meanwhile, we have designed an excellent 'import system' of our own, with the gracious help of Herr Karl Strausser.''

''Ahhh, yes, Karl....''

''We are certain, relying on the excellent information that we've received from various sources, that the quantity of cocaine we purchased through Mr. Levi will be exhausted in a very short time.

''By the time that happens we will have a clear channel to each of our coordinators with the synthetic product.''

''So, you'll have lots of dope and lots of dope users, how will this benefit us?''

''In two ways. Number one, the negative publicity campaign will be set off by the distributors, the gangs who will be undercut by our product. They are already at war in the streets, you can imagine what it will be like if they suddenly find themselves being undersold. The 6:00 p.m. news will be filled with horror stories of blues and greens that they had never heard before.''

''Blues? Greens?''

''These are gangs, sir, who control the ghetto drug trade.''

''I see....''

56

"Number two, we will actually bolster our economy with this operation."

The president edged forward slightly. "I don't know if you are aware of it, sir, but cocaine, as it is used in the United States, in its crack or rock form, offers immense profits.

"We have been informed, once again from a very reliable source, that one gram of rock cocaine sells for one hundred dollars."

"One gram?"

"Yessir, one gram, one hundred dollars."

"What is this rock that you're talking about?" Malan had to cancel an appreciative smile. Oom wasn't the president because he was slow-witted. He was glad that he had done his homework.

"Three fourths of a gram of cocaine is mixed with baking soda or some other like substance; we've been informed that powdered strychnine is sometimes added."

The president frowned his distaste. "The mixture is put in a jar or some clear container that will withstand heat. The container is placed in boiling water until the mixture coagulates. Cold water is flushed on this coagulated sphere, thus making a rock of cocaine."

"And this is smoked?"

"It is smoked."

"One hundred dollars per gram?"

"Yessir."

"And what is the effect and how long does it last?"

"We've been informed, sir, that the effect is equivalent to a very powerful orgasm and that the effect will last from ten seconds to a half hour."

The president stood slowly, shaking his head. "What fools those Blacks are! What fools!"

"Yessir, they are, and we intend to use their foolishness for our benefit."

"Carry on, Henrik, carry on."

***

Dap Sugar Charlie stared at the poster of the Jamaican woman on the ceiling above his bed.

The young woman was a Chinese/Hindu/Indian/African/Jamaican. She was standing in a pool of still water, pulling her hair back, seducing the camera. He had fallen in love with the poster, he had fallen in love with her gorgeous breasts, her lush mouth, the slinky eyes, the curve of her frame, the obvious love she exuded. She was his wake-up fix.

No matter what had happened, no matter what was happening, he always felt better when he could open his eyes and look up at Ms. Jamaica. She was his Stability-Juice.

He rolled over in his oversized waterbed and practically stumbled into the woman. He shook his head in surprise; she was an African woman, full ass-sized (he graded them—boobies, girls/asses-women) and he couldn't remember her name. He laced his hands behind his well-tailored head and stared up at the Jamaican woman.

What is this bitch's name?

It suddenly became a problem for him because, number one, he was ten minutes away from easing from under his golden sheets to go to the spa, and he had made a commitment to remembering the women he fucked.

He selected his "stock" carefully; no "strawberries" for him. They had to go through his personal physician, Dr. Cuba; which meant tests for every possible known disease. He hated the whole idea of rubbers.

"Dicks were not designed to feel in rubbers." He studied her back carefully, cautiously cataloguing the color, dimples in the lower hip region. He had reduced his "fuckin'

58

program" to "women of color," which reduced his "mistake quotient" to ten or less.

Damn! Who in the fuck is this? He replayed his previous evening back through his head-tape.

Major league drug transaction at the Foxx Club; it looked like this Peter Fonda-looking white boy was heavily off into some major league drug using. Or some major league redistributing. Sometimes it was hard to tell what people were about, when it came to coke.

Dinner at the Thai place. They waited for him to show up and redesigned whatever was on the menu to suit his taste.

"Lemme have number 14 and I want that motherfucker to burn my ass off. O.K.?"

A semi-party at Tudu Bem's house, real crazy Brazilian stuff, people dancing like they were in a trance 'n shit.

Another major league dope deal with Moses, the Peruvian dude. The motherfucker was importing more dope than a nigger had hope. And that was saying a lot.

But it all seemed like Boy Scout shit in comparison to the shit that the white boy had proposed. Hmmmmmmm. . . .

Mundina! Hah! That was her name. She was this silky sweet, semi-wealthy sister from Zaire that he had been trying to "select" from the "register" for a couple months.

"The Circuit" only admitted men and women of color who could produce the sex safe card, that precious piece of paper which said "I'm AIDS free." Everybody seemed to be willing to deal with syphilis, gonorrhea, herpes and minor league infections like that. Nobody wanted AIDS.

He watched her roll her pelvis over to him. Mundina. Yes, Mundina. They had fucked two weeks ago for the first time.

He composed himself. He became Dap Sugar Charlie, mastermind of situations.

"Ummmm, good mornin'," she said. He curled himself into a fetal knot, placed his hand under his chin and stared at her. Let's see what makes it a "good mornin'"; the evening before that placed her anonymous hips behind him on his golden-sheeted waterbed was practically forgotten.

Yeahhhh, let's see what makes this a "good mornin'." Thirty minutes later, he knew what a "good mornin'" was. Or, at least one version of it.

Well, damn the spa, I don't need to work out no way today.

He spent the afternoon doing what he usually did after he had patted the woman on the ass for the last time and sent her on.

"Dap, will I see you at the club tonight?"

"I just might be there and I just might not be there. You know how it is."

She had started to say something else before he pulled his coke vial and spoon out.

"Here, lemme give you a little getaway powder."

Mundina was gone, he had already sold six thousand dollars worth of coke and it wasn't even two o'clock yet.

He stared out the window at the ocean. Living in Santa Monica, across the street from the Pacific, tripped him out. It was like having an empire.

He could wheel 'n deal with the people east of him, in the inner city, and not feel that he was a part of any of it. It was magic, it could all be done on the telephone, or his computer.

Wonder what the white boy is about. Van Niekerk, some kinda German. Or Dutch maybe. He strolled from the window to his office.

"Van Niekerk here."

"Yeahh, this is Dap Sugar Charlie."

He mulled it over while driving east on the Santa Monica Freeway. This motherfucker wants to buy my operation and re-franchise it himself. The white boy had made it plain and simple.

"Dap Sugar, I want you in my organization, how much will it take?"

Yeah, the white boy had made it plain and simple. He needed a front man and was willing to pay major league coins to get him. The setup sounded juicy but he was going to feel on it for a couple weeks, consider the pluses and minuses.

One thing he knew already: if there was major league white money involved, he'd be dealing in millions instead of thousands. The idea appealed to him immensely. He had already come to the conclusion that Van Niekerk was probably a foreign agent. A Russian maybe.

Well, who gives a fuck? If he's talking about making Dap Sugar Charlie richer, that's what really matters.

Friday night. He flushed his smoked windows down as he made his exit from the freeway and turned south on Crenshaw Boulevard.

Friday night. The sassy fragrance of barbecue drifted up his nose.

He swallowed hard, pushing back the desire to stop for a dinner.

Nope, no charcoal in Dap Sugar's system. What sense would it make to be rich and sick?

He patted his forty-year-old belly and smiled. It wasn't as hard as it used to be, when he was serving time for petty crimes and doing two hundred situps a day, but he knew he looked good in his clothes and that's what mattered, looking good.

He slowly pulled into a parking space on the side of Page 4, one of his favorite show places. In Chicago it was "Sweet Georgia Brown's," in New Orleans it was "Lillie's Place," in New York, "Smalls." He would even trip off to Mexico City, from time to time, to style and profile in the penthouse of the Sheraton. The silent word was passed, Dap Sugar Charlie was on the set.

61

"The usual?"

"Nawww, fuck the Perry-O water, I feel like a big shot o' somethin'. You got any Tanqueray cold?"

"We could chill it."

"Yeahhh, do that. Stick a bottle off in a champagne bucket with lots o' ice packed 'round it and send it over to my table."

He turned from the bar to stroll over to "his" table, a dance area reserved fringe table, that offered him a ringside view of the sugarbuns twirling, bouncing strobe lights, drummed up excitement.

He loved being Dap Sugar Charlie. Being Dap Sugar allowed him the latitude to act as crude and ignorant as he wanted to, to be profane and pretend to want the finest, to cuss people out or make them feel special.

Dap Sugar was a beautiful front, pinned in place by cocaine.

He caught her peripherally and let her stand there for a full minute before acknowledging her presence.

"May I sit at your table?" she asked.

"No, you may not," he answered, and turned his attention back to the action on the dance floor. Women could really mess things up.

O.K., so you are this super fine bitch that I done spent last night with, and most of the morning, but that sho' as hell don't entitle you to this night too.

Mundina considered the possibility of creating a scene, but vetoed it out of consideration for her love of cocaine. Dap was the "sugar" and it wouldn't really serve any purpose to alienate a source as rich as he was. Cocaine was much more important than pride.

She leaned over as close as she dared and whispered, "Call me whenever you like."

He ignored her suggestion and focused on the waitress gliding over to his table with a bottle of Tanqueray in a champagne bucket of crushed ice.

Mundina made a graceful exit, smiling like a runaway model, grateful to be a part of the set.

"Your Tanqueray, sir."

He watched her sit the bucket and stand within easy reach, pull a frosted cognac glass from the crushed ice in the bucket.

She held the glass out to him, opened the Tanqueray and poured a couple dollops into his glass. He pinned her. Dark-skinned Creole woman, fulla Indians 'n shit.

"What's your name, baby?"

"Shebelle."

Shebelle. Shebelle. Shebelle....

Hot-eyed motherfucker. He knew her type, touch her navel and *all* of her sprang open. You wouldn't just be getting pussy, you'd have access to all of the experiences she'd ever had and more.

"Sit down, Shebelle, have a taste with me." He was pleased to see her immediately respond, disregarding customary rules, the whole nine yards.

He stared a dagger at the bartender-manager, to let him know that he was financially covering for his breach of cafe etiquette. And to let him know that he should have someone else cover Shebelle's tables.

"We need another glass. You dig Tanqueray?"

"I don't drink."

He studied her face. Fine sister, high cheekbones, low-slung eyes that made her look like she was ready to fuck in a minute, Indian nose.

"Well, what's your high?" he probed, intrigued.

"I like power," she answered, "and people who know what it's about."

He sipped a cold cognac glass of Tanqueray. This was going to be interesting.

Chapter 5

Colonel Malan made a visual sweep of the huge room, filled with the cream of Pretoria's finest. He fixed a pleasant smile on his face as he strolled to the buffet table.

A "small" gathering for the birthday of the president's youngest daughter.

He felt almost ebullient. The American operation, code labeled "Operation Cobra," was succeeding beautifully. It had only taken three months for the operation to yield excellent results.

The infiltration of the ghetto drug market with Kaltenbrunner's synthetic cocaine ("ghetto blaster") had produced the desired results. The ghetto gangs were totally at war, the evening news was dominated by the negative images of young Blacks being lined up against graffiti-filled walls, and what was happening in South Africa seemed to be obscure and far away.

Joseph Levi talked of how brisk the arms sales were going to the United States.

"It's incredible the amount of fire power these young Negroes are asking for. We had an order for an armored car. We had to turn it down, of course, but can you imagine?! An armored car in Watts?" Haifa Joe had not been the least shaken when their dope dealing stopped after the initial transshipment.

"We will have other business to do, I have no doubt of it."

Several major international corporations had put out subterranean feelers to reestablish in South Africa. Or to develop enterprises. They clearly understood what a lack of negative images meant, if no one was paying attention to the situation, money could be made.

"Henrik, come over here, we need the opinion of a well-seasoned mind in this discussion."

He responded to the invitation to join a clot of acquaintances. He knew them but did not consider any of them friends. Intelligence Agency people couldn't afford the illusion/luxury of having friends.

Greta Malan had been granted a place within the charmed circle and blew it. She had been his last friend.

De Villiers, Klerk, Ploen, Smuts, Bloomforts, Malan, old Afrikaner families, he was proud to be a member of the chosen people.

He flashed an all-encompassing nod to the group as he joined the circle. Very interesting, he observed, how subconsciously the Laager mentality works. He had noticed it many times before, how the Afrikaners aligned themselves in closed circles at most social events.

"Henrik, we were just talking about the impending release of Mandela, what do you think the primary result will be?"

He had to control the urge to frown. Why were they all focusing on one single Black political prisoner? Why couldn't they relate to the idea that South Africa was being given relatively benign news treatment? Why didn't they focus on the fact that several major corporations had sneaked back into the labor market? Where else could you have things done so well, so cheaply? The Black South African, and those others who came from neighboring states, were a diligent well-trained force. Why didn't they focus on the recent spur of the nation's gross national product? It was always Mandela or one of those other bastards.

"The primary result of Mandela's release is already being felt. Our servants are becoming cheekier, the African strolling the streets of Pretoria is less apt to turn his eyes from ours, his general attitude is more belligerent."

Several of the group nodded in agreement.

"They feel a pride that we should be able to relate to Remember how we felt when we threw off the English yoke?"

The Smuts, Johannes and Magda, ardent Nationalists frowned thickly and slugged down their whiskies.

"But Henrik, how can you compare the two experiences We threw off the English collar, yes, but we were a civilized people asking consideration from a civilized people. How can you compare us to *them?*"

"I'm not making comparisons, I'm simply supplying what I think is a truthful answer. The question was, I believe, what will be the primary result of Mandela's release. And I'm saying that we're already experiencing the primary results.'

"But the analogy of the English, the Afrikaner and them?"

"Well, let's simply say that the analogy was, its unfortunate, but we all have some idea of what it means to obtain a degree of power that you've never previously had."

Johannes Smuts reddened and signaled a servant for another scotch.

"I think you're projecting matters unrealistically, Colonel

Malan. It sounds as though you see these people, somehow, taking over the government."

"No, Johannes, heaven forbid that you would come to that conclusion from my remarks. I'm simply giving a realistic book at the primary result of Mandela's release. That was the question, was it not?"

Several people nodded in agreement.

Claude de Villiers, always one of the most reasonable, volunteered: "Well, I can't disagree with Henrik. What he says is true. I mean, we can see how things have changed. They strike, they ask for considerations they've never asked for. Yes, of course, I know the communists are behind all of it, but nevertheless we're facing a monster that no one on this room is prepared to cope with."

He nursed his second glass of Perrier, studying the faces and postures of the group.

"What should we do? I mean, after we've talked ourselves blue in the face, what should we do?"

Marta de Villiers directed the question to him. He stiffened his back and replied, "There is only one thing we can do to prevent the inevitable."

"And that is?"

"Be prepared to fight until every white man, woman and child is dead."

Johannes Smuts literally snorted his disgust with Malan's suggestion.

"Why couldn't we fight until every Black man, woman and child is dead? We did it at the Blood River."

Malan stared into Jan Smuts' liquor-reddened face, feeling contempt for the hard-headed farmer.

"The Blood River, Johannes Smuts, was a million years ago in many ways. We can take pride in a glorious history but that won't help us win a future war. When it comes we must think of an enemy twenty-six million strong, with allies all over the world."

"We have allies too, have you forgotten?" He made suave bow and eased away from the circle. There was n sense talking to Smuts or any of that type. They had the minds fixed in 1948, or 1848, and they were inflexible, deadly combination.

It seemed that the Smuts could never be made to understan that the battle had been going on for as long as they had bee Afrikaners, and they were hanging on by a thread.

He made his way slowly to the exit, there was work t be done, reports to read, a war to be fought.

He made a slight wave of goodbye to Dr. Kaltenbrunne as he edged past the bodyguards stationed at the exit.

***

Anna Viloen peered over the top of her reading glasse at the Black man. Six feet tall, dark brown skin, expensive clothes, luxury car, a bloody rich stinking kaffir.

The man had first entered her shop four days earlier looking for, as he put it, "something as valuable as my family's jewels."

She didn't relate to the expression in the way that he mean it, which caused him to laugh at her.

"And how valuable are your family's jewels?" she asked

"How valuable are *my* family's jewels?! Hahh hah hah hah hahh hah..."

After he had enjoyed a good laugh at her expense, h explained the joke involved, and expected her to share the humor of it. She forced herself to render a tight little smile in response.

"Now, then...?"

"Name is Morgan. Jimmy Morgan."

"Now that we've had our little joke, Mr. Morgan," she

hated to dignify the nigger's name with a courtesy title, but she had been told that it was necessary, to do business in America, "perhaps you can tell me what you want."

"My, my, we do seem to be a bit testy today."

"I am quite busy, sir, and I have no time for joking."

He made a theatrical gesture of looking around the shop, purposely allowing his look to linger on the two women at the opposite corner. Busy?

"Well, I have a good deal of paperwork to deal with."

It was an obvious lie and they both knew it.

His jawline hardened and the look in his eyes went from humorous to serious.

"Look, Mrs. Viloen..."

"Ms. Viloen."

"O.K., Ms. Viloen, I explained to you the other day when I walked in here..."

"It was Monday past."

"Whenever. I explained to you that I was looking for some pieces of jewelry that would have investment value. There are a number of other places that I could've gone to but I've been told that you have jewels of a rare cut, excellent quality, and that you're expensive."

She nodded in agreement, suddenly seeing another side of this Black man. Dr. Shaggers was right, "They are incredibly flexible people, almost like chameleons."

"Please step over to this counter, Mr. Morgan, we've just received two new watches from Switzerland, they are both from Anton Baguette and the price range is from $35,000 for the single hand piece to $50,000 for the double hand piece."

"Awright, now we're talking business. Incidentally, you have a very interesting accent. Where are you from?"

"Many places, a private Dutch school, a French language academy, a Swiss finishing school."

"Where are you from originally?"

Colonel Malan had warned them, "It might not be such a good idea to burden yourself with a South African passport in America. Play around it as much as necessary."

"My father is Dutch, my mother German, and I was born in Greece. Anything else you'd like to know?"

He slowly lifted the Baguette from its case and held it up in the sunlight.

"They're beautiful, aren't they?"

"Yes, they are," she agreed. He studied the faceted makeup of the jewels crusting the watch surface for a few moments.

"This is...?"

"This is the Anton Baguette Imperial and the price is $50,000 plus tax...."

"And this one?"

"The Anton Baguette Deluxe Edition, the price is $35,000. There are only four other watches of this make in the world today. One of them is owned by Prince Fuad Al-Hazri."

"Give me those prices again."

"Fifty thousand dollars plus tax for the Baguette Imperial and $35,000 for the Baguette Deluxe Edition...plus tax."

"I'll take both of them, on one condition."

She focused her most entrepreneurial look on his face. "Yes?"

"I want you to deliver them, in person, to my home, tomorrow evening."

"That, Mr. Morgan, would be quite impossible."

He opened up his nine-by-eleven briefcase on top of the counter and began to count out $85,000 in thousand dollar bills.

"I want you to deliver these watches tomorrow evening, to my home. Is it possible?"

He appealed to her perverted sense of humor.

"It seems that we shall have to bend some of the rules. What time?"

"Let's say about dinnertime?"

"I'll be there. Your address, please?"

He gave her an address on a well-known street on the Upper Northside, to her surprise.

"My receipt, please?"

"Yes, of course."

They made an effort to handle the exchange of money and receipt as thought it were a "normal" transaction.

A slight smudge of perspiration dampened the edge of the receipt as she placed it in Jimmy Morgan's hand.

"Six p.m. tomorrow?"

"Yes, 6:00 p.m. tomorrow, and thank you for coming to Viloen's."

He left her shop with a sarcastic smile on his face.

***

Claus Van Der Merwe crumbled one sheet of paper up, scribbled the beginning of his report on another sheet of paper and stopped.

How could he report to Malan that he had made a personal killing, based on insider trading? What would he think?

The disposal of drugs into the Bantustans was simple; there was a built-in market, it was a seller's paradise. He felt like a man selling water in the desert.

The problem of how to distribute Kaltenbrunner's "ghetto blaster" presented no problem. He practically had an audition to find the two best "front people" for his organization.

"Hey man, my name is 'Maddog' Billy Smith, O.K.? And I'm down for all games, O.K.?"

The 70/30 split (Van Der Merwe 70/30 "Maddog") offered each of them more than enough money to play with.

"Billy, we need a number three man."

"No problem, man, all you got to do is keep the crack coming in."

Van Der Merwe leaned over his desk once more, a determined look on his face. He decided not to mention his recent "good fortune" in the stock market to Colonel Malan.

"Dear Sir, the operation is proceeding exactly as planned. I have two dealers directly under my control who are distributing our product to the gangs in the Bantustan.

The product has been enthusiastically received, as you are well aware, and all of the suggested results are being accomplished.

"Sincerely, yours, Claus Van Der Merwe." He reread his note to Colonel Malan, to make certain that he wasn't saying anything that he shouldn't say.

Why mention that he had cleared $300,000 in "undercurrent" money? What purpose would it serve? Malan knew, obviously, that he was going to make some effort to enrich himself. The cocaine trade was strictly government money, they raked it in as though it were tax money.

He felt a little nervous as he sealed the note into an envelope. He would mail it to the Consulate and from there it would go to South Africa by diplomatic courier.

He leaned back in his swivel chair and stared out at the city below him.

It was so easy to make money in America, especially in the stock market.

***

Hans Botha listened to the message and laughed aloud. The Harlem operator was frantically signalling in their special code for more coke.

"This is Brother Bud! The meat is near the bone! I repeat, the meat is near the bone! If I do not receive a shipment by tomorrow I will lose ten percent of my customers. Brother Bud callin'."

Ten percent of his customers?! Botha laughed again. There was not even the slightest possibility of losing one percent of his customers. They were natural consumers, the Harlem crack consumers.

Dr. Shaggers was right, the American Black is prone to drug using, alcohol abuse, any kind of mind-altering substance. One only had to place it in front of them in order for them to use it. They were like rats with slices of cheese.

He had made a number of trips to Harlem, to see for himself what "the dark continent" looked like. He had received validation for all of the information they had been given.

They were a low, dirty people, totally without redeeming social traits.

He shuddered, thinking of what Johannesburg, Pretoria, or any of the other great cities in his country would look like if the Zulus took over.

They want to create Harlems, places where they will feel comfortable, dirty, immoral.

There was no need to fear them, he had come to the conclusion that all of the fuss about Mandela was a mistake. They should free him immediately and put him on the government payroll, he would probably become an alcoholic or a drug addict within a few months.

The telephone ringing jarred him from his racist reveries.

"Henry, this is Brother Bud...."

Chapter 6

Sunday, June 26, 1988, Los Angeles Times:
Cold killers and fearful innocents
Homeboys: Players in a Deadly Drama

"It's happened so many times. One of the homeboys would get back to the neighborhood all bleeding, saying, 'Awww such 'n such, they did such 'n such to me.'

"And just because I'm there I'd say: 'I be back'. Jump on my bicycle—whooom—head back to the house, get my gun, come back out to the neighborhood, go to one of the homeboy's house, put WD-40 oil down the gun, put the bullets in—click, whiiish—turn the revolver, make sure it's cool. Let's go. Get in the car, roll where we gotta go, talk about what we gon' do, park the car, walk around three, four blocks to where they at, shoot 'em—boom boom—run back to the car."

David Stewart, a former Main Street Crip, describing a

payback shooting. By Bob Baker, Times Staff Writer.

Ju Rock: "Drugs, to me, it's cool. There's a lot of people who don't have no jobs. You sell drugs to people who use it. You not responsible for what they do with it. If you don't give it to 'em, somebody else will.

"If it's up to me, I'd rather be selling dope than taking money from people with a pistol in my hand. If we're selling dope, whatever we're selling is what they want us to get our hands on. We ain't got no connections in Libya to go tell somebody we need seven hundred tons of this stuff.

"Selling drugs, it kept me from robbing. It kept me from stealing. It kept me from doing a lot of things I used to do."

Colonel Malan studied the news story intensely. He felt a positive glow. Any news item with so much negative interest about gangs and drugs was, for his purposes, a coup. It meant no news about South Africa.

"Like most gang members, he's tried his hand at selling rock cocaine. He stood out in the streets, conducted transactions, then went into the house, got the dope from the 'head man' and brought it back to the buyer.

"He was not a big timer. He grossed maybe three hundred dollars a day, kept half of it. But after a year he quit. He almost got arrested, and he was afraid of being shot."

He glanced through a few more American newspapers, pleased to see large-scale spreads on drugs and gangs, or both. Excellent.

He made a note to clip the most sensational stories for Oom. Now then, the reports: John Van Niekerk.

He sprawled back in his chair and tented his fingers under his chin. Dap Sugar Charlie sounded like a familiar name. Yes, of course, Dap Sugar was the dope peddler from the Flying Foxx. Evidently Van Niekerk had made a connection of the best with the worst. Good.

Claus Van Der Merwe sounds solid, no outstanding

75

problems.

He suspected, from reading between the lines, that Claus was having some success in the stock market, but that was to be expected. None of them were stupid and they had all been placed in lucrative positions.

Anna Viloen's report puzzled and then disturbed him. It was a bit too humorous, filled with unaccustomed snips of insight and color. He frowned. There was something wrong.

What had happened to the "Teutonic Maiden"? The solidly humorless lady. He laid her report aside for a second, more serious reading.

And Hans Botha, the racist's racist. He almost winced, reading some of his sentences: "They eat the worst kinds of foods; If you drove through Harlem on a Saturday night and smelled it, the smoke would make you sick.

"They drink like fish, there is a liquor store on every corner to accommodate their urges. If there were no liquor stores, there's no telling what they would do.

"I suspect that the census is grossly overprotective of their legitimate birthrate. I suspect that it would be closer to eighty-five percent illegitimate, if they were going to be honest.

"Our product is the most popular on the market, it thrills, excites and helps them to be normal, I think."

Colonel Malan placed the reports off to one side of his desk, to re-study at a calmer moment. He recognized a degree of "Americanization" in each of the reports, but he really felt disturbed by Anna Viloen's report. He decided to give her one more report before withdrawing her from her position.

***

Roger Cranberry frowned at the page he had just typed... "another ghetto crisis." He was sick of doing pieces

76

about "ghetto crises." It was so unchallenging.

He had almost developed a formula for writing pieces about "ghetto crises." You started off saying something in "jungle grammar"—"he done did most ever'thing," and went off into something Oxfordian.

In most cases the juxtaposition of grammars was enough to grab his editor's approval, the large, white, solidly-constructed, one-legged ex-Vietnam vet that everyone affectionately called "Master Sam."

"Sam?"

"I didn't think you'd ever cop to that Master part."

"Sam, look, why do I keep getting these "ghetto crisis" assignments? Why can't I have a little taste of the Westside?"

"Roger, you want to hear the absolutely sinful truth?"

"Yes, I do."

"You and the six other fully-qualified African-American reporters on this large white daily newspaper are being given an inordinately large number of 'ghetto crisis' assignments because I feel that you all would be the most sensitive people to deal with whatever is happenin' in those areas. I'd like to quote a line from a WWII movie—'You don't look like the enemy'. The rest of us do."

Sam bent his head back over the silly article he was reading. Why the hell would anyone object to doing stories about the ghetto? That was where the news was.

Roger stared at the top of Sam's balding blonde head for a moment.

"Sam?"

"Roger? You still here?"

"Yeahhh, look..."

Roger Cranberry fanned his hand down into his pinstriped pants.

"Well, spit it out. What's the beef?"

"It's this ghetto crisis stuff, I'm sick of it...I want...

77

"Roger, tell ya what, you complete this last piece and we'll kick you over to the beach for a couple stories. That suit you?"

"Sounds find to me. Don't get me wrong, Sam, it's not that I don't dig doing stories about the ghetto, but I don't want to be ghettoized. Can you dig where I'm comin' from?"

"I can dig it, man," Sam answered and went back to the article. He wasn't a person to waste a lot of time, energy or words.

He looked up at Roger's back as he strode out of his office and back to his desk. Wish I had about six more of him.

Roger Cranberry stumbled into the last fourth of his article, number three in a series of six, frustrated by his lack of information about the name of the latest generic brand of cocaine.

Some of his white colleagues had placed him to the Deep Right after having "discussions" about the current drug plague.

"Awww c'mon, Rog, how can you look down your nose at some poor bastard who's trying to quiet his pain? How much different is that from our three martini lunch?"

"In one way, not very different at all, but in some other ways, quite different. Number one, we can afford our three martini lunch hours because we have nice salaries to pay for those three martini lunch hours."

"But Roggg...!"

"Hold on, lemme finish! You talk about some poor bastard trying to chill his pain out? I can dig that, but why with a 'rock'?"

"Well, maybe that's the current brand of martini in the ghetto, Rog."

"Phil, you just might be right, but it's like those martinis we were talking about; nobody grabbed your arm and forced you into the Dirty Garter Saloon and I have yet to hear of

78

'crack' dealers going from door to door giving out free samples.''

"There's no doubt that there's some truth to what you're saying, Roger, but we're talking about a dude who's down at the shitty end of the stick and knows it, knows that there is a ninety-nine percent chance of him remaining down there forever.''

"Alan, I started from the bottom of the shitty stick, just like the guy you're talking about, and I've come a long way, baby. If I can do it, so in the fuck can he.''

"Yeahhh, I hear you, Roger. But let's face it, you're different.''

The "discussion" always dissolved on that note.

"You're different.'' Motherfuckin' right I'm different. I better be, if I want to survive and be whole.

"Frustrated, Mr. Cranberry?''

Big Ms. Jenkins again, the giant sister from UCLA, the ex-high scorer from the ladies' team. Horny as a middle-aged Texas steer.

"No, Mzzzz. Jenkins, just mad as a motherfucker!''

"My, my, my, such language!''

She perched on the side of his desk, all five foot ten inches of legs, hips, breasts, sexy eyes and pony tail swaying provocatively. Only the tail was phony, the sister was for real and had made it obvious and simple on at least three occasions.

They had gravitated toward each other at the Dirty Garter Happy Hour. Some of his fellow reporters accused him of "racism" because he had chosen to spend the happy hour in a corner booth with Ms. Jackie Jenkins from the ads section.

"Why haven't I seen you around here before,'' she aggressively quizzed him.

"'Cause I been hiding.''

"From me?"

"I don't think that would be possible."

"You got that right. My name is Jackie Jenkins, what's yours?"

"Roger Cranberry of the Cranberrys of Chitlin Switch, Mississippi, and I'm happily married to a hot-blooded woman from Louisiana named Crystal."

"Is she Black?"

"About three shades darker than hot chocolate."

"I'm glad to hear that."

"You are?"

"Yeahhh, 'cause if you had told me you were married to a white girl, I would pull you outta here and whip some work on you this very hour."

The second time they bumped into each other at the Dirty Garter, she had "whipped some soul work" on him.

"Heyyy, what are you going to tell your friends?"

"What friends? Those are just white folks from the job, they're not friends."

They had driven, for some perverse reason, straight to a Figueroa Street motel, complete with water bed, wall mirrors, and X-rated videos, stripped and had an orgy.

He had called a halt to the whole business after the second time.

"Jackie, we won't be able to do this again."

"Why not? You don't seem to be having any problems getting it up."

"That's not what I'm talking about."

"What *are* you talking about?"

"I'm saying...we can't get together, we can't do this again."

"Why? Because I make you come in my mouth?"

"No, baby, not because of that, believe me. It's because I'm married and being with you makes me feel guilty."

"Ohhh pleezzze, gimme a break, pleezzze!"

"Don't you understand, I feel guilty. Guilty. Guilty. I leave you and go home to my wife and I feel guilty."

"Roger, look, let me explain something to you, maybe you won't feel so guilty. I'm a big ol' fine African-American sister, what some people useta call a 'stalyon'. O.K.?"

He nodded, agreeing.

"O.K., now there ain't a whole lot of brothers out there who can come onto me and damned few white men and absolutely no chinks and spics. Now here you are, a beautiful brown-skinned six-foot hunk of a brother and you're telling me that we can't do this good thing anymore because you co-exist semi-peacefully with some woman during the course of the week. I don't want your soul, man, I want your nuts."

She placed him on the sexual defensive and kept him there. They were three months beyond their last encounter.

"So, you're frustrated, huh?"

"About this fuckin' article."

"Sounds like you're in need of a little more intelligence than you're into right now, after all, two heads are better than one. And one good head is better than anything."

She flicked her tongue out at him like a snake a few times and strutted away from his desk like a lascivious peacock.

Heads, male and female, surreptitiously studied her special parade through the office aisles. He followed the wake of stunned heads before turning back to his own problem.

What the fuck am I wracking my brain about? Dap Sugar has the answer to all this shit.

He dialed "The Flying Foxx," Dap Sugar's basic station.

"Would you have him call Roger Cranberry, area code (213) 555-5000, extension 332, as soon as he comes in?"

"Cranberry, who you?"

"Just tell him, he'll know."

The bartender, assuming a drug deal was about to go down,

81

promised to report the call.

"Remember, please, Roger Cranberry."

Two pages and three cups of black coffee later Dap Sugar Charlie returned his call.

"Dap, how's it goin', man?"

"It could be bigger but it sho' in the fuck couldn't be better."

They exchanged the slipshod banter that a couple of homeboys were privileged to exchange, twenty years encapsuled by a few coded sentences.

Dap and Roger had shared the same wine bottles, smoked the same joints, and on two occasions shared the same girl.

"Hey, blood, I didn't know you and Ginola had a thang goin' on."

"Shit! I didn't know *y'all* had a thang goin' on!"

"Well, ain't no real big thang."

One thing became painfully obvious (to Roger) by the time they reached their junior year in high school.

Dap Sugar had chosen the easy way out.

"Awww fuck, Roger! What goddamned difference do it make how you get your coins? Just so long as you git 'em!"

The difference that it made sometimes separated them for years at a time, while Dap Sugar paid his debt to society and Roger slowly climbed the city's journalistic ladder. But they remained friends and Dap Sugar was an invaluable, up-to-date reference-resource for anything happening in the city's underworld.

"Dap, I need some information, man."

"I'll give you whatever I can but it sho' in fuck ain't gonna be over the phone."

"Where do you want to get together?"

"Leave your pinstriped tie off 'n meet me over at the Stage Lounge."

"What time?"

"It's about 3:30 now, let's make it 6:00 p.m., O.K.?"

"See you at 6:00."

He felt half an urge to wander through the ads department on his way out at 5:30, to flirt a little with Ms. Jenkins, but vetoed the idea. The sister was so serious about playing that she could take a run-on sentence and slam dunk it.

***

Anna Viloen stepped from the shower, her hair covered by a peppermint-striped shower cap. She began drying her body off with a large, fluffy towel, released her hair from the shower cap.

Slowly, hesitantly, she stopped toweling her body to stare at herself in the full-length mirror. It was not something she took pleasure in, or did often.

She made an objective study of what she saw. A well-formed thirty-two-year-old white woman, an Afrikaner who could trace her tribal origin back to the 18th century. Well formed. She made a slow turn, running her hands down over her breasts, her ribs, waist, hips, buttocks.

I have an ass like a kaffir. Maybe that's what he likes.

She had always exercised, enjoyed the games that demanded maximum physical exertion, tried to reduce the size of her buttocks, but nothing worked.

Secretly, she had come to accept and believe the rumor that the Viloen males, meeting the fat-assed (she couldn't remember the anthropological name) Hottentot women on the dunes of the Cape had permanently damaged the genetic makeup of her family tree.

There was, of course, no official evidence of inter-sexual behavior, but all of the women in her family displayed signs that were unmistakably related to the fat asses.

She placed her heels together, stood at attention with her

83

hands on her hips and stared into her deep-set gray eyes.

In thirty-two years two males had penetrated her body; her Uncle Frank... "Come, beautiful Anna, give your uncle a kiss," and her father, "If you tell anyone about this, Anna, God will be very angry with you."

She turned abruptly from the mirror, wrapped a beach towel around her nakedness, snatched up a brush and began to savagely give her lustrous black hair one hundred strokes.

She stopped after ten strokes and turned to stare at her image again, tears in her eyes; first my uncle, then my father, and now a bloody nigger wants me. God must really hate me.

***

Roger Cranberry studied the scene, "pinstriped tie" left in the glove compartment of his Datsun 210.

The Stage Lounge. The usual collection of slick types, a couple tables filled by well-dressed Black women who had obviously decided to get together for a gossip session over funny drinks with miniature umbrellas hanging onto the edges, a Stage Lounge mixture.

He catalogued an odd habit, maybe a Stage Lounge custom; each person entering was ignored until he/she settled in place and then they were closely scrutinized.

He knew, from having been on the scene before, that most of the regulars knew that he was tight with Dap Sugar Charlie. They kept records on things like who related to who and why.

He sipped his gin and tonic, wishing it were a glass of the Beaujolais Villages he and Crystal had picked up from Trader Joe's a few days ago.

"Sweetheart, there's just one thing you just gotta tell me before we... before we... before we..."

"Say it, Roger, before we get married."

"Yes, Roger, I have had sex with other men, six to be exact, just as you have...."

"Naw, fuck sex! I wanna know why your folks named you Crystal."

"That was my mother's idea. For some reason, while she was pregnant, she developed this craving for Brazil nuts. I'm sure she never ever thought I'd be hooking up with somebody named Cranberry."

They had settled on a nickname—"Miss Baby."

The bartender caught him smiling into his drink.

"We got another one just like that."

"Good, lemme have it."

He drained his glass and prepared to deal with the next one. Six-fifteen. Oh, well, he knew better than to expect Dap Sugar to be on time.

**

"Anna, glad you could make it...c'mon in!" After two visits to his home she still stood in the door, feeling vaguely awkward.

The first dinner, her delivery of the Baguette watches flashed through her mind. Cornish rock hens and wild rice, braised leeks, an excellent white wine. He had been charming, humorous and warm. She had left feeling slightly confused, a feeling she attributed to the after dinner cognac and espresso.

She felt no urge to return but couldn't turn down an invitation "for a small gathering, people who have shown some interest in my watches. I think your business will benefit and besides, they're all pretty nice folks."

Jimmy Morgan had been the only Black at the "small gathering." Three couples, well traveled, intensely intellectual; a playwright, the president of a prestigious small college, an architect, two astrophysicists, "We just couldn't resist each other," a film producer.

The problem of South Africa was tabled in favor of the Israeli-Palestinian conflict.

"Well, I have to say, honestly, as a semi-Zionist and a quasi-religious Jew, that I think the Israelis are way off the beam, and have been for some time. They remind me of a couple bulimics I used to know, the more they eat, the more they think they have to eat."

Jimmy Morgan, the perfect host, had not taken any position, he just simply kept the hors d'oerves trays full and the wine flowing.

When he pecked her gently on both cheeks at the end of the evening and asked, "Are you O.K. to drive? I mean, we don't want any accidents happening, do we?" She had assured him that she was fine and left, feeling strangely nauseated. No Black man had ever been close enough to her to kiss her. Black women, nannies, had cooed and fondled her, but a Black man, never.

And now she was back, a third visit, to offer him her judgment of a few pieces of jewelry he had purchased ten years ago. Or so he said. "I'm pretty certain I got taken on this deal, but I'd really like to know how badly."

She followed him, walking like a shop window mannikin, into the large room he called his "den."

There was a fire in the fireplace, cognac on the long marble table in front of the sofa, facing the fire. Exotic music drifted out from somewhere.

"Where are the pieces you want me to look at?" He turned to look at her, an amused gleam in his eyes.

"I have them upstairs. Can I offer you something?" She stared at the cognac bottle and into the fire for a moment.

"Yes, a drink would be fine, thank you."

He poured her a drink, poured himself one, handed her

the snifter and offered a toast: "Here's to our friendship."

They touched glasses and sipped in unison.

"Make yourself at home, I'll be right back." He placed his glass on the table.

She watched him stride from the room and wandered closer to the fireplace. How many rooms were in the house? What did he do for a living? Where did he get his money? Who was the woman in his life?

A Black, a kaffir, a nigger. She gritted her teeth together and felt like throwing her glass into the fireplace. What the hell am I doing here?

She had had ugly dreams for a couple nights after her attendance at the "small gathering." No one had openly suggested that she and Jimmy were "together," but the implication was clear. What other reason was there for her being there? Alone....

"Business," she muttered savagely and sipped her drink.

She could easily imagine what her friends back in Pretoria would say about her being in a Black man's house, socially.

"Anna, never!"

"I love fires too."

"Ohhh!"

"Sorry, didn't mean to frighten you."

"It's alright, I was just thinking about...well, never mind. You have the jewels?"

He held a nine-by-eleven velvet-coated tray up in front of her.

"Right here. Where do you want to look at them?"

"The table would be fine."

She placed her glass near his and took her jewel glass from her purse. He undraped the tray and sat next to her on the sofa as she adjusted the glass in her right eye.

He had several necklaces, a few rings, two pairs of pendant earrings, a bracelet. She could tell at a glance that they were excellent pieces, well cut.

"I need to know how much you paid for each piece before I give you my estimates."

"Be right back."

He moved quickly to get pen and paper. "Alrighty, now then, lemme see...the necklaces, $30,000, the rings, $10,000. The earrings, $8,000 and the bracelet was $15,000. That comes to $63,000."

"And these were purchased from a reputable merchant?"

Once again, the amused gleam appeared in his eyes. "Leewanhoeks, Amsterdam."

A reputable dealer, indeed.

She began to study the jewelry. Jimmy Morgan leaned back on the sofa and studied her.

***

Dap Sugar Charlie glided through the door, a couple recent toots of high-grade coke zinging through his frontal lobes, coke macho evident in every motion. He didn't do it often but when he did, he used the effect to the maximum.

The Stage Lounge, three fourths filled with the late afternoon set, stared at him as though he were a celebrity. In a sense, he was.

"Brother Cran! What it is?! What it is?!" Roger had already fortified himself against Dap's boisterous onslaught. He knew he was going to have to endure a first-stage level session of loud talk, outrageous behavior and too much camaraderie before they settled down to second-stage level talk.

"How you doin', Dap? You lookin' good."

"Hey! When you lookin' good, you feelin' good, ain't that right, y'all?!"

He addressed his question to the Stage Lounge at large

and received a half-throated chorus of affirmation.

"Heyyy!" he boomed out again, "I said when you lookin' good, you feelin' good! Ain't that right, y'all?!"

The two tables filled with the sisters who were drinking umbrellas chorused back, "Yeahhh, you got that right!"

"Waitress!" he bellowed out, "give them beautiful sistahs over there whatever they want!"

Roger laughed aloud. Dap had done it again. No one could jack the atmosphere of a place up higher than he could. Or as fast.

He mounted the stool beside Roger, enjoying the hyped-up ambiance he had brought into the place.

The bartender leaned across to him, anxious to serve.

"Lemme have a Perry-O in one o' them fancy snifters. And stick a fresh slice o' lime off into it."

"Dap, you O.K., man? Perrier and lime?"

He was slowly comin' down to stage level two. "Never felt better in my life, swear fo' God! but that's because I'm takin' better care of myself than I used to. Hey! What's happenin', dog balls?!"

He spun on the stool to greet a fellow thug. And turned back to his monologue without a pause.

"I got hip to myself during that last little bit I had to do, you know, behind that dumb ass real estate scam me 'n Patchass tried to pull off. I said to myself, now wait a minute, Dap Sugar, you damned near forty fuckin' years old. You done drank all the ignunt oil you ever gon' need, you done smoked kilos o' dope. You done dropped all known varieties of pills 'n shit. You done even shot a li'l heroin, quiet as it's kept."

"Really?! I didn't know you had gone that route."

"For about six months. I'd get a li'l taste and get high but I soon eased away from that, I couldn't afford to be strung out.

89

"Anyway, I just decided to see what the other side looked like."

The bartender made a ritual of depositing a round napkin and his cognac glass of Perrier on the bar. Dap laid a hundred dollar bill on the bar.

"This is for everything."

"So, you mean you don't do anything nowadays?"

Dap Sugar smiled at his homeboy and draped his arm across his shoulders affectionately.

"Now hold on, Cran, let's not get too serious. Shit! Too much of anything is bad for you, even too much good health. I'll toot a couple lines every now 'n then...."

"That's what I wanted to talk to you about." Dap, off on his personal litany, ignored Roger Cranberry's would-be interruption.

"I'm not above smokin' some excellent 'erb, but it's got to be damned good. I'll suck up a li'l Tanqueray from time to time and I sho' in hell ain't gave up good pussy."

"What's good pussy, Dap?"

"That's pussy what's got claws 'n suction cups up in it."

They reached the lower level of stage two and he was on his favorite subject,

"Mannn, I pulled a young sistah, one of the waitresses, outta Page 4 the other night who is supernaturally fine. Speakin' o' fine! How is yo' wife, man? Now that's what I call fine—Crystal."

"She's doin' great. I called 'n told her I was getting together with you and she told me to invite you over for dinner, anytime."

Roger felt Dap Sugar stiffen and watched his eyes go from warm and gleaming, talking about women, to hard, brilliant.

"'Scuse me, Cran, be right back."

He watched him slip through the clots of people and place his catcher's mitt-sized right hand on the back of a man's neck. He whispered a few words into the man's ear and pushed him toward the exit-entrance.

"Uhhh, Dap, I don't want to get into your business, but what was that all about?"

"The usual, money. That motherfucker been owing me eighty-five hundred dollars for the last two weeks. I gave him two more days to come up with it or else face the consequences."

"Eighty-five hundred dollars?"

"Yeah, 'n got the nerve to be hanging out on my set. He's lucky, if you hadn't been here I'd a kicked 'im in the ass. How y'all doin', ladies!?" he suddenly turned to shout over his shoulder to the two bubbling tables at his rear.

"We doin' fine, baby! Why don't y'all come on over here?!"

He made a casual wave neither accepting nor rejecting, and turned back to Roger.

"Her name is Shebelle, man, one of them dark-skinned Creole women, you know, the ones that look East Indian 'n shit. Got them slow burning eyes and them high cheekbones, gorgeous turd cutter on 'er."

Roger felt pure admiration for Dap Sugar's proven ability to deal with so many diverse elements at one time. Man would've made a brilliant lawyer.

"Yeahhh, brother, I got to be really careful about this one. She don't smoke, don't drink, ain't never been married or had no babies. And when I got my report from Dr. Cuba, he told me that she was practically a virgin. Can you imagine that?! A twenty-four-year-old semi-virgin?!"

"That is kinda hard to swallow."

"I ain't havin' too much trouble."

They shared a laugh, enjoying each other's company.

"Now then, what's this about this coke thing you wanna talk about?"

91

"Coke thing?"

"A few minutes ago you tried to interrupt my flow when I was talkin' about tootin' every now 'n then."

"Oh yeah, well, what I wanted to know is . . ."

"You eat yet, man?"

"I had lunch."

"Awww shit, that was this mornin', c'mon, follow me over to this little Thai place I know. Them motherfuckers be *doin'* it with some noodles 'n shrimps. We can talk better over some hot peppers."

Roger almost stumbled to the floor climbing off the bar stool.

"Damn! My foot went to sleep on me."

"Bullshit! That gin went to your foot, that's what happened."

He turned and laid another hundred dollar bill on the bar and gestured to the two tables of partying sisters.

"Get 'em drunk, man, don't let any one o' 'em outta here sober."

The bartender nodded solemnly, dutifully.

"You goin', sweet thang?!" one of the sisters called out, slurring.

"I'm goin' right now, baby, but Dap Sugar Charlie will return."

Chapter 7

She removed her glass, took a sip of her cognac. The fire had warmed it to a fine point.

Jimmy Morgan looked at her, a look of casual expectancy.

"Well, Mr. Morgan..."

"Jimmy, Anna, Jimmy," he corrected her.

"It seems that you're the winner of this deal. The cutting of the stone for the necklaces and the bracelet is exquisite. They show the work of a master. Do you have any idea who it was?"

He shrugged nonchalantly. "Who knows?"

"In any case, in my opinion, your total investment is easily covered by the necklaces and the bracelet."

"How's that?"

"Well, what I'm saying is that the necklaces and the bracelet are easily worth $100,000. You can, of course, get someone else to look at them but..."

"Anna, I wanted your opinion, not a consensus."

She tried to ignore the fervent sound of his statement.

"I think, in addition, that the stones in three of the rings could be re-cut, to enhance their aesthetic appeal and value. In any case, I can say without hesitation that you are way ahead of the game with those pieces."

He nodded, sipped his cognac, appeared to be bored. She stood up, prepared to leave.

"Now then, if there's nothing else that you'd like me to evaluate for you..."

He looked over the upper rim of his glass as he spoke to her.

"Anna, sit yo' ass down and stop actin' like a fuckin' freshman in a Catholic girl's school."

The tone of his voice settled her back down onto the sofa.

***

The waitress and the owner of the Thai restaurant greeted Dap Sugar's flamboyant entrance with gracious smiles. He was, obviously, one of their favorite patrons.

Roger Cranberry, slightly high from the gin 'n tonics at the Stage Lounge, almost enjoyed Dap's manner of speaking, a kind of bullish roar to all of those who weren't within half a yard of him. And sometimes to those within a half yard of him.

The assorted collection of diners, several whites, a Black couple, a few Thais, seemed to scurry for some kind of emotional shelter as they listened to his dominant strains.

"You new here, sweetheart, what's your name?"

Roger studied the extensive menu as Dap struggled to pronounce the waitress's six-syllabled name.

"O.K., *that's* enough o' that, we'll call you Ahhh, O.K.?"
The tiny Thai waitress, notepad and pen in hand, smiled

shyly.

"O.K., your order, please?"

"Where's Somluk?" he asked in his stage-one level voice.

"Somluk in kitchen," the waitress answered.

"SOMLUK! C'MON OUT! I KNOW YOU'RE IN THERE!"

The other patrons looked at the two of them, puzzled, a bit pissed with the disturbance, but more curious than anything.

A tiny Thai woman, her mouth wreathed with a smile, a spatula in her right hand, popped out of the kitchen. She quick-shuffled to their table and accepted Dap's lascivious hug.

"How you doin', Momma-San?"

Mama-San? Momma-San?!

She disentangled herself as quickly as she had popped out of the kitchen and quick-shuffled back to the kitchen, the smile widened by four inches.

"That's my girl," Dap explained, and cast a gracious smile around at the people who were looking at them.

Cranberry nodded, understanding. Dap Sugar made no distinctions between races, except when it came to sex.

"Hey, let's face it, man. Ain't nothin' different 'bout one man or the other, we all git a hard on. But me, I kinda like climbin' up on top of a dark woman, or a brown woman. Or a yeller woman. You know what I mean? I ain't got nothin' 'gainst white women 'cept that they make me think of snow 'n snow don't make my thang feel excited. Can you dig where I'm comin' from?"

"What're you gonna have, Dap?"

The waitress reappeared, almost mysteriously. "Take your order now?"

"Yeahhh," Dap sounded off: "We'll have number 1, 2, 3 and 4, to start off with. And then number 15, 18 and 12.

95

And let's start off with some o' that good Thai beer y'all got. And make number 15, 18 and 12 hot. I want some pepper feeling off in there!''

The waitress scribbled furiously for a few moments, took their order and quick-shuffled away. Roger felt slightly overwhelmed by his "host."

"How did you know what I wanted?"

"Easy. It's got to be 1, 2, 3, 4 or 15, 18 or 12. Or something else. And if you don't want none o' this good Thai beer, you a freak or a fool."

Roger sprawled back in his seat, at ease for the first time in a week. Dap Sugar Charlie was like a breath of fresh air. Or a jolt of new brand cocaine. The waitress poured their beers.

"Your food will be here shortly," she said.

"It better be, else we gon' start nibblin' on you," Dap answered.

She scurried away.

"Now then, what about the coke question?"

Roger Cranberry gathered himself in. What did he really want to know?

"The word is out, Dap, it's something else. What is it?" Dap Sugar Charlie lowered his voice, went to stage three, his we-got-secrets-to-share tone.

"It's called 'ghetto blaster', brotherman, and it is completely addicting. The first time you smoke it yo' ass is hooked. You hear me, the first time!"

They mauled number 1, 2, 3 and 4, interweaving four Thai beers.

"Hey, man, I can see why this is your favorite restaurant. I'll have to bring Crystal over here."

In between courses, they talked about "ghetto blaster."

"What makes it so different from the usual stuff?"

Dap Sugar stared into the distance, uncharacteristically

96

meditative, a stuffed chicken wing on its way to his mouth.

"That's a toughie, blood, that's really a toughie. All I know is that you can't fool around with the shit. You can't do nothin' with it but leave it alone."

Roger was dying to ask him if he was dealing in it, what the economic turnover was, who was importing the stuff, but decided to cool his hand, wait for the right moment.

"Dap, I read somewhere that they had performed an experiment with monkeys. They gave them unlimited access to cocaine. One monkey pressed a bar 12,800 times to get a single dose of coke."

Dap Sugar paused as he scooped up a forkful of pad Thai.

"Did you say 12,800 times?"

"That's right, 12,800 times. They found that Rhesus monkeys won't smoke tobacco or marijuana, but one hundred percent will smoke cocaine, preferring it to sex and to food— even when they were starving."

Dap Sugar shuffled his shoulders, a nervous gesture for him.

"Yeah, that coke don't be fuckin' around."

"How does 'ghetto blaster' compare to 'ordinary' coke?"

Dap pursed his lips, red chili juice in the left corner of his mouth.

"Let's put it this here way: If that fuckin' monkey you talkin' about would be willing to press a bar 12,800 times for one dose o' coke, he would press that bar 'til all his fingers wo' out for a dose of 'ghetto blaster'."

They sipped their Singhas in unison. Now was the time.

"Where does it come from, Dap?"

Dap Sugar Charlie, extralegal entrepreneur, hustler, drug peddler, woman lover, looked seriously puzzled.

"I don't really know, home. I really don't."

Friends, they had a deep respect for their friendship. Dap Sugar furnished drug, crime, "subterranean" information.

Roger Cranberry returned the favor by giving Dap tips from the "square" world. "They gettin' ready to run a sweep through South Central next week, Dap. If I had anything cookin', I'd turn it off for awhile."

Roger Cranberry cast no moral aspersions at Dap and Dap kept most of his opinions about Roger's square lifestyle to himself. They bridged a lot of gaps with their friendship.

"You have no idea?"

"Not the slightest. You want another brew?" Dap Sugar felt vaguely ashamed. How could he tell Roger Cranberry, his partner from the joint-in-the-park days that his script was being written by a weird-ass white boy in Malibu?

***

She stared at the honey-brown chest of the man sleeping next to her. So smooth, almost hairless.

She laced her hands behind her head, oblivious to her nakedness, and stared up at the beautifully cut chandelier above their bed. His bedroom.

Two cognacs, three, four, a kiss. She thought she would vomit when he pressed his lips to hers and gently squeezed her breast. A bloody goddamned kaffir was kissing her. Her father would've dropped dead at the sight.

Her father. A dry, bitter smile creased her mouth. My father. My uncle. Colonel Malan. The last thought almost jerked her body erect. Colonel Malan. My mission.

Jimmy Morgan watched Anna Viloen's reactions to some kind of secret stimuli under hooded lids, pretended to be asleep. What the hell was this beautiful woman going through? Maybe she was having second thoughts about having sex with a man she had only known for a short time. He decided to ease the demons away.

"Good morning, Anna."

"Good morning, Jimmy," she responded stiffly.

"Did you sleep well?"

"Yes."

"Are you...do you feel...do you think we did the wrong thing?"

She turned to face him, to look him full in the face, to stare at the nappy hair, the dark face, the brown eyes, the wide nose, the thick, delicious kaffir lips, the odd smell of his armpits.

"Yes," she answered, "yes, we did everything wrong!" and pulled herself into his surprised arms.

***

Crystal "Miss Baby" Cranberry suavely filled her husband's wine glass half full of Beaujolais Villages...their "nightcap" for this particular evening.

"From the cute li'l beer smell on your breath, I don't really think you need this, but if anyone is gonna cause you to have a hangover, let it be me. Cheers!"

They touched wine glasses and took sips. The sister was so real. He stared at her as though he were seeing her for the first time. After two years of marriage complete with an overview of his sexual thrusts at Ms. Jackie Jenkins and her mistake with a D.J. whatwashisname?, he loved her more than he had when they first got married.

Nut brown, corn rowed, bright, almost too fine, a perfect reporter's wife. She understood late no-show dinners, missed appointments, was absolutely flexible.

"Roger, c'mon, honey, you're a reporter, don't try to make me feel guilty because I'm not going to weep because you're not going to be home at 6:15 p.m.

"Wowww, Roger, looks like Dap Sugar, with his sweet self, took you on a trip through his wild, wild underworld kingdom."

She forced him to "de-burden," as they had coined the term for lifting the world off of each other's shoulders.

He was able, after a fashion, when she eased the problems of the psychotherapist's life into their marriage, to "de-burden" her shoulders. But, he had to admit, she was better at it than he was.

"Is it that obvious?"

"If I showed you a mirror, you might be tempted to remodel the creases in your forehead."

They shared, exchanged a smile of understanding.

"Baby, you know what?"

"No, what?"

"I think Dap has turned me onto something I don't really want to know about."

She was familiar with his distaste for the "crisis in the ghetto" series.

"I don't quite follow, pass it by . . . real slow . . . ."

"They're selling a new kind of cocaine . . ."

"Oh my God! Not more cocaine . . . ."

"I said, a *new* kind of cocaine. And it's not something that's distilled from coca leaves in Colombia, Peru, Bolivia, the usual places. That was bad enough. This is something new and ten times more addictive. Dap says you can't even try it or else you'll be hooked."

"And he doesn't know where the source is?"

"That's what he says, and I believe him."

"What do you make of it?"

"I don't know. The whole situation has an odd flavor to it."

"You think someone has done a designer number on cocaine?"

"That's a possibility. But who?"

He took a long sip of his Beaujolais and tried to pull off

100

a lascivious wink.

"Why don't we deal with that manana? Right now, we need to feel on each other's bodies."

The prolonged kiss that they exchanged (fleshed out by three gin 'n tonics, four Thai beers and a glass of Beaujolais Villages) left Roger Cranberry snoring on their waterbed and his wife smiling as she watched a few minutes of the late, late news.

Everything was gangs, gang violence, cocaine "rock" trafficking, drive-by shootings; what the hell was going on in South Africa? When were they going to release Nelson Mandela?

***

Roger Cranberry, "Cran" to Dap Sugar and a few other old-time friends, dialed "Master Sam's" extension for an appointment, a mere formality for the "In" people.

"Roger, stop this fuckin' nonsense 'n bring your ass on in here."

Roger Cranberry, the reporter of things happening in the ghetto, was requesting a stay.

"I can't really put my finger on it, Sam, but I'd like to follow it through."

"What about your westside beach yearnings?"

"We can get back to that later on. Right now I want to track down some crack."

"What do they call this stuff?"

"Ghetto blaster."

"Wowww!"

"Yeahhh, that's what I said. I know dope names can become real satirical, but that sounded ominous to me."

"I think you got a point. O.K., check it out. We can drill it in behind the "ghetto crisis" series. You know, it's really funny about these drug things, they can lead you into some strange corners. Be careful, Roger.''

He strolled past sister Jenkins, a new perfume reeking from her cleavage, his head throbbing with a serious hangover, his mind on one question—where did the ''ghetto blaster'' come from?

''Good mornin', Mr. 'Glandberry','' she called to his back, trying to be funny.

''Oh, good mornin' to you, Miss Jenkins,'' he replied.

Chapter 8

Colonel Malan replayed the tape of his conversation with "Mr. Smith," his C.I.A. liaison.

"We are seriously concerned about the efforts of one Roger Cranberry, a reporter on the Los Angeles Vista, to gather information about the influx and source of the new cocaine called 'ghetto blaster'.

"We are aware that he has an excellent opportunity to trace this drug to its origin and we are expressing concern about this matter."

"Mr. Smith, I can assure you that you will not be identified with this matter in any shape, form or fashion."

"We will not be, Colonel Malan, rest assured of that. And the Director of our agency asked me to convey that thought to you."

"Thank you for conveying the thought, Mr. Smith."

"You're welcome, sir, goodbye."

"Goodbye."

He replayed the tape again, trying to read between the lines in "Mr. Smith's" voice. Was he trying to tell him something? Why would the C.I.A. become anxious about an operation that was as successful as "Operation Cobra"?

He realized the usual anxieties were at work, at a fever pitch now because Mandela was being released.

The weak hearted were becoming spineless, as indicated by the number of "flyaways" and "deserters."

And the strong were entrenching. He numbered himself and his president as members of the latter group.

"I'm quite pleased with the results of 'Operation Cobra', Henrik, quite pleased."

"Thank you, sir."

Why wouldn't he be pleased? "Operation Cobra" was bringing dollars into the government treasury, a surefire disinformation campaign was off and running and several multinational corporations, previously leery of dealing with them, had sent out feelers for readmission, through third party sources.

But all was not well. The developing problems stemmed from his clairvoyant notions about the performance of his coordinators.

Van Niekerk's reports were coming in late, sloppily put together. Botha was threatening to blow his cover by becoming prominent in a fringe lunatic, racist, neo-fascist party. Claus Van Der Merwe appeared to be steady, but was becoming a bit too interested in making money for the sake of making money. And Anna Viloen had become a ripe question mark.

He leaned back in his chair, seriously considering a quick "beef up" trip to America. He was forced to veto the idea immediately. Too much to do at home.

All of the security systems were on the alert, every possible agent at work. They had their hands full, trying to prevent the ANC and other radical groups from stirring up twenty-eight million Africans to give Mandela a welcome home celebration, a celebration that would overwhelm minority rule.

***

Anna Viloen ignored the messages.

"This is Ramona, please contact Ramona as soon as you receive this message. Repeat, please contact Ramona as soon as you receive this message."

She clicked the machine off and sat staring at it.

Ramona was her westside distributor, Maurice was her southside distributor, and they were both frantically trying to reach her, to make their connection for the next shipment of "ghetto blaster." They had money waiting to be picked up.

She stared at the machine. She shuffled a few papers from one area of her desk to another. She felt ambivalent, lousy. She placed her palms against her temples and squeezed. She had made love with a Black man.

The images of them in bed together caused her to shake her head from side to side, like a rogue elephant in musk.

Oh my God, what have I done?!

"Ms. Viloen? Ms. Viloen?!"

Mildred Court, one of the "Viloen's" salespersons, stared at her boss' strange actions.

"Are you all right?"

"Yes, of course, the cramps, you know how it is."

Mildred Court acknowledged the problem with a sympathetic shrug.

"I know what you're going through. . . ."

"What was it you wanted, Mildred?"

"Oh, a messenger brought these for you."

Anna Viloen looked at the trio of American Beauty roses and felt like screaming.

"Thank you, Mildred."

"Would you like something to put them in, Ms. Viloen?"

"Yes, thank you, Mildred."

She held the roses in her hand as though they were cobras about to strike. Mildred Court scurried back into her office with a coke bottle.

"This is all I could find."

The salesperson quickly arranged the flowers in the bottle.

"There. They're really beautiful."

Anna Viloen nodded in agreement, numbly. A half hour later she walked quickly out of the store, leaving instructions in her wake.

"Mildred, close up for me, will you, dear?"

"Yes, of course, Ms. Viloen."

The two salespersons exchanged curious expressions, watching Ms. Viloen stride north, past the shop's window.

Darlene, the synthetic blonde, whistled in surprise. "Wheeewww! That's a new one. I didn't think she knew how to leave this place before midnight."

"Cramps, you know how it is."

The salespersons exchanged empathetic looks and continued looking the way chic salespersons in high-priced jewelry shops on Michigan Avenue were supposed to look.

Anna Viloen crossed Michigan Avenue, striding purposefully toward the lake.

She felt bewildered. She wanted to cry, grit her teeth with rage, scream, stop someone and pour her heart and guts out.

The boats in the marina, the calming motion of the lake relaxed her tension somewhat. She sat on the giant rocks fronting the lakefront, thinking.

***

"So, you think it's kinda odd that I should be wealthy, huh?"

"I didn't say I thought it was odd; I just asked a simple question because I was curious."

"Well, let me answer your curious question. The Morgan money is inherited money. You look shocked."

"Do I?"

"Yes, you do. Should I go on?"

"Please."

"Grandmother and Grandfather Morgan put the fortune together. Granddaddy buried Black bodies when no one wanted to touch them and grandma catered Louisiana goodies to rich white folks. They put their money in real estate, mostly, and, strangely enough, jewelry. I think that was grandma's idea. She had this weird notion that 'diamonds last forever', or is it, 'diamonds are a girl's best friend'? In any case, my parents took the ball and ran with it."

"Took the ball and ran with it?"

"They multiplied what was passed on to them."

"Your grandparents, are they...?"

"Dead as doornails, both of them, but living in the Morgan Foundation."

"It's remarkable."

"What's remarkable about it?"

"I mean, a Black family...?"

He cast his familiar amused look in her direction.

"Anna, we don't have thousands and thousands of rich Black people in this country, as you well know. But please be aware of the fact that we've always had a few superfortunate Blacks. I count myself in that bunch. I've always had everything I wanted; the best schools, travel, cars, clothes, whatever. And, as you can see, I ain't no mulatto

107

either.''

She folded her hands in her lap. A nigger has fucked me. Her mind played with the thought for a couple beats. And I fucked him back....

She wiped her hands across her eyes, trying to redesign the images flickering through her consciousness, redesign the future.

He was gentle, he was intelligent, he was good looking, he was wealthy, he was Black. She didn't want to con herself into seeing a future for them.

What future could they have? She was a South African secret agent established in America to distribute ''ghetto blaster'' to the Bantus. Would he send her roses if he knew that?

They were passing in front of her before she fully realized they were there; a mother, father and two children, Blacks, strolling along the lakefront.

''Hello!'' the children sang out, skipping past.

''Hello,'' she replied mechanically. The parents smiled and nodded pleasantly. Blacks were everywhere, and they gave no evidence of being subservient.

She turned to watch their lakeside stroll.

Kaffirs...niggers...Jimmy...

She felt the warm rush of tears flowing from her eyes before she fully realized she was crying. She covered her eyes with her hands, trying to stop the flow.

The mother, a forty-two-year-old veteran of the blues and other emotional wars, moved toward her with her arms outspread to embrace her.

''We're Christian people, honey, and we felt that we had to come back and offer you some comfort, you looked so sad and lonesome. That woman has some serious problems, I said to my husband, some serious problems.''

She enveloped herself in the Black woman's arms, tears

streaming unchecked, sobbing.

***

Van Niekerk divided the money into two piles, one for himself and one for Dap Sugar Charlie.

"There we are, $30,000 for me, $20,000 for you." Van Niekerk gave a surreptitious, contemptuous look at Dap's flamboyant clothes, the trio of gold chains around his neck, the diamond earring in his left ear, the chartreuse shirt and designer jeans, the crudeness of his language.

"Where's it comin' from, Kneechurch?"

The question, coming at the conclusion of their latest bit of business, rattled him slightly.

"The name is Van Niekerk, Dap, Van Niekerk. I've explained that to you before."

"Hey, man, I can't be pushin' my tongue outta joint tryin' to remember how to say a bunch o' foreign names 'n shit."

"You like the money that foreign names have, don't you?"

"I do my share to get it," Dap snapped back. The two men glared at each other for a moment, the vague hostility developed over the months breaking the surface.

Van Niekerk made a diplomatic decision to defuse the situation.

"Yes, Dap, you're certainly right, you do earn what you're given."

"You still didn't answer my question."

"I'm afraid I can't, it's against company policy."

Dap Sugar made a face and stuffed his share into a black silk gym bag.

"Well, I guess that's it for the moment," he said and walked from Van Niekerk's gallery office.

"Uh, Dap, just a minute, please. Allow me to give you a little tour of the gallery, it'll look good in case we're being

109

watched.''

"You show me these fucked pieces o' shit every time I come here.''

"Please, just in case.''

Van Niekerk, as irritated with Dap as he was with him, made a serious effort not to lose his temper, in turn, he slowly strolled along the east wall of the gallery.

"We have something new, a work by a Black artist, you might like it.''

They paused in front of a large charcoal drawing of an overweight, Aunt Jemima-looking figure, bent over a number ten tub, washing clothes on an old-fashioned scrub board.

Dap cocked his fists on his hips and sneered.

"What the fuck is this supposed to be?''

"Well, obviously, a Black woman washing clothes.''

"Why in the fuck don't she take 'em to the laundromat?''

"Let's assume that they're not her clothes, she's taking in washing for a living. She's doing her job. The point is how well the artist has captured the moment.''

"This ain't sayin' shit to me, Kneechurch, all I can see is a sister slavin' in a tub fulla hot suds.''

Van Niekerk was forced to smile at his remarks. "Well, let's step over here, tell me what you think of this.''

"You say a Black artist did that?''

"Yes.''

"He must be from the last of the Stepin' Fetchit School of Art.''

Van Niekerk ignored his comment and led him to another large portrait, a surrealistic work by Kan Tangay, entitled "One Half of a Migraine.''

Once again Dap cocked his fists on his hip and sneered.

"What're you sellin' up in here, man?''

"This is one of the finest of the modern surrealists.''

Dap frowned at the slashes of weird colors, the discarded

110

gym shoes melting on the head of a miniature pony, the manic figures running in a circle at the top half of the work.

"How much you charge for something like this?"

"The artist wants $80,000, the gallery will get sixty percent of that."

"Eighty thousand dollars?! For this?!" Dap blinked in comic relief, "Eighty thousand dollars for this?!"

Van Niekerk laughed. This was really a funny guy, once he stopped being the most cold-blooded drug dealer in the ghetto.

"That's the going price."

Dap shook his head from side to side.

"Man, you know something, you gettin' over like a fat rat."

"I assume that means something good."

"You fuckin' A right it does."

Dap Sugar held his hand out for Van Niekerk to slap, a gesture he had learned to respond to almost by accident.

There was something almost primitive, almost childish about the slapping of hands, like children playing in a sand box.

"I gotta get on. What's it look like for next week?"

"You'll be receiving the usual package on Monday. Incidentally, how are matters going with the gang leader, you were having a few problems with him about the cut."

"No problems. I put his ass back in gear right quick. No one wants to derail a gravy train."

Van Niekerk surprised him by saying, "I heard that!" in a caricature of the slang language.

"You know something, Kneechurch, you awright. I mean, you got problems 'n shit, but you awright. . .for a white boy."

"And you're alright for a Black boy."

Dap's quick frown was slowly replaced by a wide smile.

111

"Later on, man."

"Yeah, later."

***

Roger Cranberry made his way through the maze of desks, responding to a summons from "Master Sam."

An obstacle named Jackie Jenkins attempted to blindside him with a double dose of "Nights in Gardens."

"Roger, how do you like my new perfume?"

He sniffed quickly, like a dog cataloguing a piss stain. "I think it's provocative, be careful."

"Where are you going in such a rush? I want to talk to you."

"Not now, Jackie, I got business to take care of, later, O.K.?"

He carried the image of her pout to the editor's door. I oughta introduce her to Dap Sugar Charlie.

"You wanted to see me, Sam?"

"Yeah, c'mon in, close the door."

Hmmmmm. . . it looks serious, he wants the door closed.

Sam stood for a moment, to scratch his pants out of his crack, and sat back down. Roger stood easily, his hands jammed into his pockets.

"Roger, how would you like to do some beachfront pieces, you know, the effect of salt water on the kneecaps, that kinda thing?"

"I thought we had already agreed to that, just as soon as I finish this last 'ghetto crisis' piece."

Sam Walters, the editor's editor, shot his hand through his thinning blonde hair, uncharacteristically nervous.

"Why don't we just let the last piece die a natural death?"

"But I'm two pages away from the end of the thing and I have some incredible new stuff to add."

"Like what?"

Roger told him about his conference with a "ghetto informant" who had told him about a new brand of cocaine called "ghetto blaster."

Walters toyed with a ballpoint, pursed his lips and squinted up at Roger. "Rog, there's something funny going on here. I don't know exactly what, but there's something funny going on. Have a seat."

Something really serious, he was asking him to take a seat. Cranberry waited, puzzled. What the hell was going on?

"I'm asking you to keep what I'm saying to you under your hat. O.K.?"

Roger nodded in agreement.

"I got a call last night, at home, from a guy named 'Smith' who explained that he was calling on behalf of a government agency."

Cranberry frowned. The C.I.A.? F.B.I.?

"He made a request that we drop the last of the 'ghetto crisis' series, in the interests of national security."

"What did you say?"

"I laughed in the bastard's face and hung up. It had to be a practical joke. That's all I could think. But then, this morning, I got a call from 'Mr. Smith's' boss. It's no joke, they want us to end the series right where it is."

"I don't believe this! Since when did government agencies get interested in local stories, pieces about South Central El-A?"

"It does seem kinda weird, doesn't it?"

They stared into each other's eyes for a pregnant moment.

"So, you want me to stop right where I am, huh?"

Sam Walters stared at the picture of his wife and sons, to the left of his desk.

"No, no, I don't. I want you to get to the bottom of this. I want you to find out why this agency is so interested in

113

closing this story down. There's no telling, you might have your pinkie on something bigger than the both of us.

"Since they've expressed an interest in having the 'ghetto crisis' squashed, I'd suggest you go low profile on it but stay on it, that should spring something loose."

"It still doesn't make sense, government agencies trying to kill a piece about the ghetto. What do you think?"

Sam Walters shrugged, making an offhand remark, "Maybe one of the biggies hasn't been keeping his nose clean, you know what I mean?"

"Oh wowwwww!"

Roger walked out of the editor's office feeling a bit spacey. Why were they interested in the ghetto? Was it the ghetto series, or were they interested in him?

"Roger, you want to have lunch with me, I know a beautiful little Japanese place..."

"It smells seductive, Jackie, absolutely seductive."

"What?!"

Chapter 9

Colonel Malan crushed the newspaper into a ball.

Damn it! The stupid fool Botha had been arrested, along with a dozen other members of the "New Aryan Circle," for killing two Black men who had stumbled on them playing war games in a secluded forest area.

Damn it!

He literally trembled with rage. The stupid fool! Why couldn't he realize that he was accomplishing more for his cause, in his role as "coordinator," than he could ever achieve by involving himself with a bunch of minor league Hitlers?

He paced back and forth in front of his office window mentally playing out a scenario.

There was a very slight possibility that Hans Botha would somehow disclose information about the real reason for him being in America.

It hardly seemed likely that anyone would believe anything a Neo-Nazi said, but he immediately made a decision to have Botha "terminated."

He paused to look down at two Black workers on the office lawn. Van Niekerk was doing an excellent job despite his sloppy reports. Claus Van Der Merwe was also doing good work, was making money on the side and had been infected with herpes by a redhead in his office building.

Anna Viloen was missing. He studied the movements of the two men on the lawn. What were they planting? Where was Viloen? Had she defected? Been kidnapped? Why were they planting so close to the entrance?

He braced his knuckles on the window sill, intrigued by the energetic movements of the two men. They didn't seem to be the usual, slow-moving Black wage slaves.

He glanced at his watch, 12:15, lunch time. The trickle of people from the various agencies in this building had suddenly become a stream.

The two Black workers began to walk away from their work, again moving more energetically than usual.

He followed their movements until they disappeared around the corner of the building. His eyes swept back to the holes they had opened on both side of the walkway. They had left their tools.

The two bombs exploded just as he moved away from the window. The blasts shattered the windows of his office, spraying his back with shards of glass.

He lay on the floor for a few minutes, watching the bloody circles form from cuts in the back of his head, his arms and back. It was best to stay in place for a few more minutes, in case they had placed another one, designed to catch the investigators of the first two blasts.

He cringed, listening to the screams of those below. The vicious, bloody, ANC terrorist bastards have done it again.

***

"Jimmy, I must see you, is it possible?"

"You sound really upset, what's wrong?"

"I can't talk about it on the phone."

"C'mon over."

"See you in half an hour."

She sat on the sofa, staring into the fire, trembling. "Anna, are you sick, what's the matter?" He gently put his arm around her shoulders.

Her eyes were glazed and puffy. She had cried herself dry on the lakefront, cradled in the Black woman's arms. She looked into Jimmy Morgan's eyes and tried to speak.

"Heyyyy, take it easy. Whatever it is, we'll deal with it. Let me get you a drink. Cognac?"

She nodded yes and stared back into the fire.

My life is ruined. How many lives have I ruined?

He placed the cognac snifter in her hand, tipped his glass against hers in a silent toast and leaned back on the sofa, waiting.

"Jimmy, there are some things I have to tell you, but I must ask you to be patient because I have no idea how they will come out."

"Why not take your shoes off, stretch yourself out. Here, lay your head in my lap. That's it. Now then, why not start at the beginning? That's always a good place to start."

The beginning?

"I was born on a large farm..."

"In Greece?"

"Please, Jimmy, if you interrupt I won't be able to say what I have to say...."

"Sorry, go on."

"A large farm. My family was not rich but we could afford

117

many workers and servants because they could be hired cheaply. My life was quite carefree until I was about nine years old.

She paused to take a long sip from her glass. "When I was nine years old, my father came to my room one afternoon while I was taking a nap and had sex with me. He told me that God would be angry with me if I told my mother, or anyone else."

He stroked the side of her face.

"Poor baby."

"He continued to do things to me, on and off, for a . . . a long time. Then, when I was eleven or so, my uncle also began to do things with me. By the time I was fourteen I had not been kissed by a boy but I had been used like a, like a seminal spittoon by two men."

The sound of a burning log settling into another position made her pause.

"I was so angry with myself, so angry with them, that I thought of committing suicide many times. My anger and shame caused me to become introverted.

"I believe my mother must have known why I was so silent much of the time, but my father was the absolute master of our lives and she could say nothing. It was the same with my uncle. They were the masters and the rest of us were the servants.

"I lured an older man into a marriage in order to get away from the situation; he was forty and I was seventeen. He drank heavily and beat me. When he drank he beat everyone, me, the servants, everyone.

"I thank God we didn't have children. He was murdered by one of the servants three years after we were married. It was only through the grace of God that he was killed by someone else because I was planning to do it. Not a pleasant story, is it?"

118

"Life can be hell at times."

"I sold the farm he left me, took the money and moved to the city. Life began to open up for me; I enrolled at a very conservative university and, within a few years, I had a degree in geology and I was recruited by the government for special projects."

Jimmy Morgan tried to conceal his annoyance. The story had too many gaps in it. Hadn't she told him she was born in Greece, that she had gone to a Dutch school, a French school/language academy, a Swiss finishing school?

She sat up slowly and turned to face him. "Jimmy, everything that I've told you up 'til this evening has been a lie."

"I don't understand. Why?"

"Because I'm an Afrikaner and I came to this country . . ."

"You're a what?"

"I am from South Africa and I was sent here by my government."

"You're a spy?"

"No, I'm not a spy."

"Well, what the hell are you? What're you doing here?"

"Please, please, I can't speak about it now, give me a little time, please."

She placed her glass on the table and turned to embrace him. She could feel the tension in his body as he recoiled from her.

***

"Now, that's what I call a beautiful dinner, thank you, Mr. Cranberry."

"You're entirely welcome, Miss Baby. I told Dap that I was going to bring you over the first chance I got."

"I'm glad you did. 'Scuse me while I redo my lips."

He watched the looks of admiration follow his wife to the ladies' room. No doubt about it. "Miss Baby" was a choice item. She was beautiful, intelligent, and had that special charm that some women are gifted with.

He contrasted her with Ms. Jenkins. God! Where in the world did that woman find a perfume that smelled like Old Spice after shave cologne, with a dash of magnolia mixed in?

"What're you smiling about?"

"I was just trippin' on how nice it is to be going home with you."

She clicked a lascivious glance off at him and threaded her arm through his as they walked to the Datsun.

"Sweetheart, did we kill the last of the Beaujolais?"

"Completely. You want to pick up a bottle?"

Trader Joe's. They made a quick work of the selection, no need to wander through the Yuppie-infested aisles, admiring unsalted nuts and bread (no preservatives).

He had decided to let his lady in on what was happening, she was not a fragile item who would faint because she knew what her man was facing.

"Something kinda weird is going on."

"That's what Sam said."

They exchanged street garb for their evening at home, black silk pajamas for "Miss Baby" and a blue terrycloth robe for Roger.

"Roger, you want a piece of cheese with..."

"Yeah, that would be great."

He thumbed through their video collection. "Seven Beauties"? "Donna Flor and Her Two Husbands"? "Ramparts of Clay"? "Black Girl"? Osmene's masterpiece, "Playtime"? Jacques Tati's beautiful comedy. "Miss Baby" closed off the indecision, entering their bedroom with a tray of cheese, French bread and wine.

"Let's see what's on the news," she said.

Professional newshawks, they dismissed the fluff and zeroed in on the lines in between.

"Twelve white men are being held for the alleged murder of two Black men. The alleged crime was committed in a secluded sector of Barnshall National Forest. One of the men is reportedly a South African citizen. Connie?"

"Two powerful bombs were exploded in front of the Ministry of Order and Justice this afternoon, in Pretoria, South Africa, killing thirty people and injuring sixty other persons, all white. This is the fifth such attack this week. No organization has claimed responsibility for the latest attack."

Crystal remoted the commercials off.

"What do you make of the Barnshall Forest story?"

"Bunch of fuckin' fringe lunatic creeps who call themselves The New Aryan Circle. Story is that the two brothers were hiking through and stumbled upon these idiots playing war games, in preparation for the upcoming race war, they killed them in cold blood. What I'm curious about is the Afrikaner. How did a Boer get in there?"

They exchanged significant looks as she turned the sound back up, commercials over.

"Twelve gang members were gunned down by a rival gang this afternoon, at least six innocent spectators were also wounded. Eight of the gang members are dead, four in serious condition. The conditions of the innocent bystanders vary from critical to stable.

"We'll have more on this story later in the evening. Jim?"

"Connie, the Los Angeles Police Department made a five million dollar drug bust today. The street value of the drugs is reported to be between ten and twelve million dollars."

"I can't stand any more, let's see what the Interview is tonight."

Crystal clicked through the channels.

"Oh my God! That bastard!"

"No, leave it on, let's hear what the latest b.s. is." The Interview, one of their few favorites on commercial TV, was being obviously quickly thrown together with the Information Minister of South Africa.

INTERVIEWER: "Are you saying, Mr. Kruger, that the recent rash of exploding bombs, people being killed, is simply the work of a splinter group?"

KRUGER: "Absolutely. We broke the back of the major terrorist organizations in our country two years ago, when we instituted our fifth State of Emergency measure."

INTERVIEWER: "We have information from sources indicating that the recent activities are being staged to demonstrate that all of the major organizations are alive and well. And that these attacks are being stepped up as a prelude to Nelson Mandela's release.

"Would you care to comment on that?"

KRUGER: "What is there to comment on? You have gangs of terrorists running around blowing up innocent people. We will not release Mandela if this continues...."

"Crystal, go around the channels real slow, I want to see something."

She gave him a curious look and remoted from channel 2 to 13 and back to the Interview.

"What? What're you looking for?"

"Hmmmmm, I don't know. I just thought about how curious it is that we should be on the verge of having one of the most incredible things that ever happened, the emancipation of twenty-eight million Black people in the twentieth century, and it's all being upstaged by gang killings and crack dealings."

INTERVIEWER: "But wouldn't that be a backward step, sir? All of the indications we have at this point clearly show that your country is in for a bloodbath if reforms are not immediately instituted.''

KRUGER: "We are a sovereign nation, I must remind you, and we will not be coerced into doing anything against our national interests by communists or other outside forces."

INTERVIEWER: "We're not talking about outside forces, sir . . . ."

KRUGER: "I'm aware of the forces that you speak of, sir, and we will not allow them to gain control of our government. Your government must surely understand how vital it is that a democratic arsenal be maintained in the region. The communists will certainly gain more power if we are left to battle them alone. The communist menace . . ."

"Well, that's enough of that, he's hit that scratchy part of his record."

They sipped their wine thoughtfully, Roger nibbled on a piece of cheese.

"Roger, you know something, as soon as the African people come to power in South Africa, I want to go there to live."

He stared at her, curiously.

"Why?"

"Well, number one, it's going to be one of the most interesting places in the world, psychologically. I mean, look at what we've been watching for years; a lot of insane white men sitting in front of television cameras, trying to justify slavery into the twenty-first century. Hell! It wasn't even justifiable when it was first started.

"And then we hear people like Winnie Mandela, and others who make so much sense that they seem superlogical."

"You got a point, Baby. They are superlogical, they've been forced to become that way. I see superpeople being designed."

"That's it, brother! You've put your finger right on it!

I want to go and look at what supermen and superwomen look like, close up."

"We've always been the superpeople, in my book, for having survived the Middle Passage and thrived. Now we're looking at people who've been kept in a slave ship in their own land."

"That's heavy, Baby, really heavy."

"Would you be willing to go with me?"

"You think I'd let you go that far without me?"

They interlinked their arms and sipped their wine.

"Baby, why don't we put on some tender music and listen to each other's heartbeat?"

"That all?"

She glided away from her seat in front of the television to select a tape for their system.

"I haven't heard Miles Davis in a while, how about 'My Funny Valentine'?"

"A lovely choice."

She clicked the system into play, turned the tulip bedside lamp to low and slowly unbuttoned her pajama top.

He stood and pulled her into his arms. "Brazil nuts, huh?"

"What if she had had a craving for all-day suckers?" They laughed quietly, enjoying their "in" joke, and sprawled on top of the bed.

***

The rising sun made a spectacular splash on the dying embers of the fire. Jimmy Morgan slumped against the back of the sofa, an arm's length from Anna Viloen, a sodden cognac-drunk fogging his senses. It was his turn.

"I wasn't attracted to you because you're white, take my word for it. What I was attracted to was a woman that I felt I had a great deal in common with. Yes, I was attracted to you physically, but I think that's to be expected; I mean, after all, you're not an ugly person.''

He paused to take a long sip of cognac. "There is this beautifully designed woman who owns a jewelry store, who must be wealthy or else she couldn't afford to own an exclusive jewelry store, right?''

He didn't wait for her response. "Which means that I wouldn't be dealing with a gold digger, if I decided to get serious about anything. My dad spent years warning me about gold diggers.''

Anna pulled the edges of the blanket around her shoulders, seeking security rather than warmth. "I was impressed by your sense of business, you know, that no-nonsense thing that you have.''

Anna forced her mouth into the caricature of a smile.

"I had no idea of what was going to happen between us, to be frank. I had no preconceived notion that we would simply fall in bed, none of that. I feel I was operating on a grander mental scale than that.

"I knew, after you had given me a truthful reading/estimate of my family's jewels...yes, Anna, there are such things...that I could trust you. And that is what real love is built on. Right?''

She nodded, agreeing, shivering slightly. "And now you bring me this fantastic story of being a goddamned South African agent who's been responsible for distributing dope in the ghetto.''

"Truth can often be stranger than fiction.''

"You can say that again.''

He swayed to his feet, lurched over to the window and tilted his face to the sun.

"I was going to share my life with you, Anna; after I had consulted my attorney, of course, Granddad's recommendation for any emotional step.''

He laughed sarcastically.

"And what the hell was I planning to share it with?"

He turned to face her.

"A goddamned South African maniac, a person who had been sent over here to poison my people."

He took three drunken steps towards her and made a wild kick that landed against her arm.

"Get your fuckin' crazy ass out of here before I get my gran'father's gun 'n shoot you! I may be a weird, booshiee-ass nigger to a lot of African-American Black folks, but I'm still aware of what the deal is."

She didn't move for a beat. He kicked her again, in the side. She rolled over and wobbled to her feet.

"Jimmy, please let me explain . . ."

She made an attempt to grab him around the neck. He pushed her back.

"Anna, the best thing I can do for you is allow you to escape. And you better hurry up and do it before I really go off."

She stumbled toward the door, too hurt to cry. She paused at the door, "Jimmy, I know how you feel," she said, "I think I would feel the same way if I were you."

He responded by throwing his cognac glass at her head.

Chapter 10

Shebelle strode from the kitchen, a fully-loaded breakfast tray on her head.

Dap Sugar sat up in bed, staring at the sight of his approaching breakfast with curious delight. Shebelle Makonnen, he had gone from Zaire to Ethiopia.

"Damn, sweethang, if you had done something like that down at Page 4, you'd a made a hundred dollars a night in tips."

She smiled slyly, "I was making close to two hundred a night, just using my two hands."

"Well, 'scuse me, ma-dame."

He watched her gracefully slip the breakfast tray from her corn-rowed head, dipping to lay it to his left side. She sat beside the tray.

"What we got here?" He "washed" his hands with fake relish.

"Exactly what you asked for, grits, eggs, toast, salmon patties..."

"That's salmon croquettes, baby."

"Salmon croquettes and espresso."

She buttered a piece of toast and held it up to his mouth. He bit.

"You know something, Shebelle, I thought you was a Creole when I first met you."

She held the demitasse of espresso out to him.

"A Creole, what's that? Aren't they very light-skinned people?"

"Naw, not always." He attacked his grits with a forkful of salmon croquette. "Nawww, not always. They got some Creoles down in Naw'Leans that's real dark, but some of 'em got green eyes 'n Japanese hair."

She took in every word as though he were a master teacher and he liked the feeling it gave him. Home-grown sisters could be so off-brand sometimes; the African woman gave a man respect. Shebelle artfully took a piece of toast, pinched off a snip of croquette, dabbed it in the grits and popped it in her mouth.

"Why don't you get another fork?"

She laughed. "We don't use forks where I come from. We eat with bread."

"You eat with bread?"

"Mostly. I'll have to make you an Ethiopian dinner one evening soon. You would love wot."

She laughed again, almost spilling the coffee. He loved to make her laugh, but he was never certain what was going to make her laugh. She had such an "abstract" sense of humor. The whole thing, to him, was "abstract."

"Wot is delicious, it's hot, you'll love it," she said, after completing her laugh cycle. It went, he noticed, from a devilish smile to a soprano/Coltrane solo. He loved it.

He had had real problems, literally, understanding where she was coming from. The only thing he knew about Ethiopia was/is that they were always on Sunday night evangelist's telecasts, starving to death.

"Ethiopia," she proudly stated one evening, "was never a starving nation until the Western influence took hold. We were always poor, according to Western standards, but we were not starving. My family, the Makonnens, were relatives of the Emperor, Lord bless his memory, and we were members of the elite class.

"I had never known anything about hardship until my family was forced to flee the Marxists."

He finished off the last of the croquettes as she swayed into the kitchen for more coffee.

Elite? Marxists? Ethiopia? He made a mental note.

"Coffee was born in Ethiopia, Pop," she announced, as she poured another demitasse.

"Oh, really?"

"Yes, really. The beasts stole it from us and transported it to Latin America, where they could import it more cheaply. But the best coffee still comes from my country."

She sat on the side of the bed again, looking into the distance, remembering. He sat the tray on the floor beside the bed and studied her profile.

The chick could be Jewish if she wasn't the color she was, he thought, with that question mark nose. Beautiful lady, filled with real live stuff. He settled back into his oversized pillows and burped.

She turned to him and smiled.

"Dap, your people, our people, are so strange here. I used to think that I would never understand them."

"Do you understand them now?"

"I think I do, about as much as they understand me."

Shebelle . . . Shebelle . . . Shebelle . .

129

She didn't have a fantastic body, or ass. And her legs looked like they belonged to an anemic teenager, but she was forcing him to explore sectors of his Africanity that he had never realized before.

"What makes you look so sad, Shebelle?"

The tears flushed themselves from her eyes, almost without a change of expression. "I feel sad, Dap, because I am not at home, because I'm not surrounded by people that I share a history with. Forgive me, Dap, but I must say..."

"Speak your peace, baby," he said solemnly.

"I feel sad about our people here, our African people. I'm not one of those stupid Ethiopians who would rather relate to the Italians or the Israelis before I relate to our people here.

"I feel very sad because I see our people drinking and using drugs, and ruining their opportunity to become the great leaders of our African world."

Beads of sweat popped out of Dap Sugar Charlie's forehead as he folded her into his arms. He seriously thought about asking her to leave immediately. If not sooner.

***

Roger Cranberry propped his heels up on his desk, rereading the story. It would've been just another story for a lot of people, but for him, and a few others, it was very, very interesting.

Crystal Cranberry called him, an unusual event.

"Roger, did you read the story on this Viloen woman, the South African jewelry store owner who killed herself?"

"I'm reading it now, I don't know what to think about it."

"See you later, how about some fish for dinner?"

"Suits me."

They were intensely interested in everything happening in South Africa. It was either South Africa and/or Jesse Jackson.

He pulled his heels off of his desk, flung the newspaper on his desk and roughly rubbed his eyes.

The "ghetto crisis" story about the latest brand of crack cocaine was going nowhere. He had developed no new leads, nothing. Dap Sugar Charlie had become a dry well.

And Sam Walters had received another call, from a "higher up."

"Roger, you're on to something, stick with it, but be careful, the bastards know something we don't know."

Whatever the "bastards" knew, he'd like to know. He tripped for a moment.

What kind of connection could there be between the Nazi who had been caught in Barnshall Forest and the South African jewelry store owner who had killed herself? Was there a connection? No, there couldn't possibly be. That was what one of the "South Africanists" had labeled "South Africanitis," an addiction to any suggestion about anything happening in South Africa, no matter how remote.

Curious, he had tried to use his news sources to find out something about Hans Botha, the South African, who had been swept up in the net that had gathered in eleven other members of his "sect." Nothing.

His news nose opened, he phone-probed for some info about Ann Viloen, the South African-born owner of "Viloen's," the chic jewelry store. Nothing. He couldn't even find out where she was born in South Africa.

Sam Walters on the horn.

"What's it look like, Roger?"

"I'm not gonna say black, let's say bleak, at this point."

"I'm a little surprised, Rog, I would've bet anyone that you were going to have the ragged ends sewed up by now."

Roger smiled. Very clever, Sam...jam the winner, cool it on the loser. Sometimes, with some reporters, you can win much more with vinegar than you can with sugar.

"Give me a couple more days, Sam, just a couple more days. I may be able to put a well-sewed three-piece suit in your lap."

"Make me a believer. Bye."

It didn't make any sense. The gig guys were hammerin' his editor about a simple ass dope story.

"Roger Cranberry, I'm pregnant."

"What?!"

"Ahhhah! So, that's what I have to do, huh? Shock you into recognizing my presence."

He bent over the papers on his desk, trying to look busy.

"Don't play games with me, Jackie, I got problems to solve."

"Like what," she challenged him.

He stared up at her, hating and loving her persistency.

"You really wanna know, huh?"

"I'm not into asking idle questions."

"O.K.," he glanced at the news item dealing with the suicide of the South African jewelry store owner, "how do I find out why this woman killed herself?"

"What woman?"

"This one!"

He pushed the story in front of her. She read it. "That's easy, check out the dude. Or the dudes who were in her life."

He felt himself reeling backwards in his chair for a second. Of course, that was the answer for her motivation. Or it could be. But what the hell did it have to do with drug distributorship in South Central El-A, with "ghetto blaster?"

"What's the matter, Roger, you going through the change?"

"Nawww, just got a lot on my mind. Thanks for your help."

"You're welcome."

He watched her flounce away, leaving a new scent behind.

Wonder what the hell that is.

He spent the next hour tracking down possibilities, running up dead-end streets.

"Dap, this is Roger..."

"Can't talk now, man, I'm busy..."

"Let's get together on the weekend."

"Yeah, cool. Later."

"Later."

Who was he wrestling into submission at two in the afternoon? Oh, well.

He stared at Anna Viloen's crude passport photo. A Boer gets involved with a native-grown Nazi group, kills two Black men. A Boer woman, a successful business person, the owner of a chic jewelry store on Chicago's Michigan Avenue, commits suicide. No connection obviously.

The C.I.A. or the F.B.I. or somebody was trying to intimidate the paper into not pursuing the end of a story about crack in the ghetto. No connection.

The reporter's curiosity-instinct grabbed control after fifteen minutes of sluggish thinking.

"Bill Forster, please, this is Roger Cranberry of the Los Angeles Vista."

A half hour later Roger sat at his desk, tapping a #2 pencil against his desk top, almost as much in the dark about why Anna Viloen had killed herself as he had been before.

And what the hell does it matter? I'm supposed to be trying to find out why they want to stop this story and where "ghetto blaster" comes from. Damn!

Bill Forster, a fellow reporter for the Chicago Beam, had been as cooperative as possible.

"Been reading your "ghetto crisis" stuff, Cranberry. Good work."

"Thanks."

"What was it you wanted to know about the Viloen

woman?''

"Why did she commit suicide?"

"The story we got from the employees in her store is that she was depressed. One of the women said that she was having bad menstrual cramps."

"Bad enough to commit suicide?"

"Hey, who knows? I'm completely outside that circle."

"Who was the man in her life?"

"A guy named Jimmy Morgan, well-to-do exporter/importer, a Black guy, incidentally."

"That right?"

"Yeah, third generation money, too."

"How did he figure in?"

"Nothing we could connect. They had only recently got together, sexual relations once, nothing deep or longstanding. Far as the cops are concerned, it's an open-and-shut case of a woman with the cramps who decided to swallow too many pills. Happens every day."

"You got a point there, Bill. Well, thanks much, buddy...be talking to ya. Oh, what was the boyfriend's name again?"

"Jimmy Morgan."

"Thanks."

He impulsively decided to get some air, take a drive down into the real world, see what he could see, hear what he could hear.

He made a right on Figueroa and headed south. He always felt a little depressed the minute he passed Martin Luther King Drive. For some reason he would inevitably always spot a depressing sight; the police searching a couple teenagers, their hands up, their legs spread-eagled.

Today it was the sight of a teenaged prostitute standing midway in the block, her left leg flexed provocatively lasciviously sucking her thumb and winking at passing cars.

Dap Sugar had informed him that this was a new breed.

"These is 'crack, rock' 'hoes, Cran, some people call 'em 'strawberries'. They'll do anything for a piece of the rock."

He took the passing scene in peripherally. He had done a series the year before about the storefront churches in the community. The year before that he had done another piece on community organizations. He felt he knew his beat pretty well.

Got to get together with Dap Sugar this weekend, see what he knows.

The two teenagers racing across the street in front of his car surprised him. Why were they running? What had they done?

Wowww! I'm beginning to think like a white cop. Anytime you see a Black man running, he must be up to no good.

He watched them match stride for stride. Brothers run like greyhounds. There was no one chasing them, they seemed to be running for the sheer fun of it.

He made a left at Manchester. Life was always on the front burner in South Central "El-A."

Wonder how the brother got hooked up to a white chick from South Africa. That would make a human interest piece alright. What was his name?—Morgan.

He turned right on Central Avenue, drove for a few blocks, stopped to get a beer.

"You got a Heineken?"

"All beer there, in there!"

Korean liquor store owners had acquired a reputation for rudeness. Maybe they didn't realize they were being rude.

He pulled out a large Rainier Ale, ("green death" a ghetto wit had named it), slammed a dollar bill down on the counter as hard as he could and walked out.

"Your change, you have change!" the store owner called after him.

"Fuck you, motherfucker!" he called back. If you wanted to play rude, I can teach you some rude.

He pulled into the north side parking section of Will Rogers Park, smiling to himself as he thought about how puzzled the owner must be. They think we're all crazy anyway. Fuck it!

He left his jacket in the car, rolled his shirt sleeves up and strolled around the tennis courts, just another dude with a brown bag of "green death."

The tennis players presented a mixture of bizarre and superb. The bizarre duo slammed the ball into the net, hit "home runs" at each other, raced around the court laughing and falling. They were obviously not trying to develop their backhands.

The couple in the next court, a middle-aged man and a teenaged boy, probably his son, slammed and whipped the ball back and forth across the net with surgical strokes.

He strolled over to a nearby bench, fascinated by the almost professional quality of their playing.

Have to get back out on the court again. Maybe I can persuade "Miss Baby" to pick up the racket.

He made a peripheral study of the six teenagers who slouched into view, fifty yards to his right. They occupied positions on a picnic table, four boys and two girls.

They seemed unusually subdued, he thought, for Black teenagers. And then he saw the reason why, they were smoking "ghetto blaster," casually passing the pipe from mouth to mouth, pausing to refill it from time to time.

They were totally absorbed, oblivious to him, to the sun, to the police circling the park, everything but the drug.

He felt a wild urge to race over to them and knock the pipe out of their hands, lecture them on the evils of dope addiction.

They'd probably stomp my ass into next week.

136

A few minutes later they drifted away, shadowy figures, off in search of more dope.

God, what a terrible way to waste your life. From one hit to the next. He left the can on the bench and decided to drive back to his office. There was work to be done.

Messages: "Dap Sugar Charlie."

"Dap, Roger here, what's happenin'?"

"I just wanted to get back to you, I was tryin' to get that third nut when you called."

"I heard that. Listen, man, I need to get together with you, there's something I need to find out about, soon."

"This evenin'?"

"This evening is cool. Where?"

"I was thinking 'bout checkin' Marla's out this evenin', me 'n my lady."

"About nine?"

"Let's make it ten, I got a li'l business to take care of."

"Ten p.m. at Marla's."

"In a minute!"

Chapter 11

They had made cautious arrangements to avoid the possibility of being "tapped." Van Niekerk had sent Claus Van Der Merwe a coded telegram, instructing him to call from an unfamiliar place, and gave him the number to call, a Mexican restaurant on Highway 1 with a private telephone booth.

Eight-fifteen p.m. Claus Van Der Merwe was punctual.

"Where are you calling from?"

"Don't worry," he laughed, "we're safe. I've rented a room in a small hotel downtown, very discreet. No one could possibly wire this place. It's perfect."

"You've gotten the news about Hans and Anna Viloen?"

"Yes, of course, what the hell happened?! Have you received anything from the colonel?"

"Yes, I have, but one thing at a time. Hans made the dumb mistake of hooking into an ultra right group..."

"The Aryan Circle."

"Right. The colonel is afraid that he may say something embarrassing. He wants to have him terminated."

Van Niekerk strained to hear Van Der Merwe's reaction.

"Terminated, you say?"

"Yes, I was instructed to tell you that he must be terminated, as soon as possible."

"But how? He's in jail."

"Claus, don't talk dumb. It doesn't matter where he is, there is someone near him who can be paid to do the job."

"I think it can be arranged."

"Good. Now then, as far as Viloen is concerned, good riddance I say."

"She was never one of your favorite people, was she?"

"Not really..."

"That paper makes a connection between her and a kaffir. What do you make of it?"

"I can't begin to imagine what they were doing together. My guess is that it was for business. She was such a cold fish."

"Yes, you're right."

"The colonel has informed me that there will be no replacements for the two of them, their regions will be left to the gangs..."

"I've read about eight murders already. They're trying to re-channel. My kaffir here in Harlem is trying to double his package so that he can subdivide for other areas. I have to keep tight reins on him."

"Well, we know how they are. So, how are things in New York otherwise?"

"I have no complaints. It isn't Pretoria or Jo'burg, but interesting nevertheless."

"One thing more, from the colonel. He asks that we make a greater effort to discredit the terrorists operating at home."

139

"They're doing a pretty good job already, blowing things up all the time. He was wounded, wasn't he, in the attack on the Ministry?"

"Minor cuts. He's a tough old Trekker, as you well know."

"Yes, he is indeed."

"Well, that's it for now. If you have anything to tell me or a question, call my gallery and we can figure out the next place to talk from."

"Good. Goodbye."

***

Marla's Memory Lane was beginning to hum a little louder, the voices punctuating the hum were becoming a little more musical.

It was ten-fifteen p.m. Dap Sugar Charlie made his entrance, pausing in every point of lighting on his way to "his" table.

His lady, a lyrically constructed sister with a Cleopatra profile, followed, two steps behind, an amused expression on her face.

Roger waited until he was settled in place, drinks ordered, friends called to across the dance floor, his presence established, before he made his way over to his table.

"Bruh Rog! Bruh Rog! What it is?! What it is?! Pull up a seat and cop a squat!"

Roger Cranberry sat down. The lady was even more beautiful up close, an Ethiopian, from the look of her nose.

"Shebelle, this is one of the few partners who survived the ol' 'hood, this is Roger Cranberry, Shebelle Makonnen."

She shook hands. She was beautiful and warm, he could tell, from her full-fledged handshake.

"What you drinkin', Roger?!"

140

"A li'l gin 'n tonic."

Dap gestured imperially to their waitress.

"Bring this brother another gin 'n tonic."

"What're you havin'?"

"I'm back on this fuckin' Perry-O Water. And Shebelle don't drink, so I guess we coulda just bought us a canteen and we'd be happy, huh, Sweethang?"

Roger detected something other than Dap's usual look of lust when he affectionately touched Shebelle's chin. She definitely dug him.

"Uhh, Dap, I have a big favor to ask of you."

Dap was reaching into his inner breast pocket before Roger completed his sentence.

"How much you need, blood?"

"Nawww, no money, man. Some info. Could we go somewhere quiet for a minute?"

"C'mon, follow me. Shebelle, I be right back."

"Nice to meet you, hope to see you again, Roger." She spoke in a soft, musical voice.

"Same here, take it easy."

They made their way through the semi-crowded room.

"Let's have some path here, Dap Sugar Charlie comin' through!"

They walked out to the parking lot in the rear.

"C'mon, let's sit in my ride, we can listen to a little music while we rap."

Dap led him to a white- and gold-trimmed Jaguar.

"Wowww! When did you get this? I thought you had something else last time we were together."

"I lease 'em, man, and I got a place that deals in exotic shit. Can you dig it?"

They mopped fives.

"Damned right I can dig it."

Dap popped an old Charlie Parker tape into the system

141

and settled back, a serious look on his face.

"Now then, what's on your mind?"

"I wouldn't rush you into this, keep you away from your lady 'n all, if it wasn't important."

"Hey, Cran, you my partner, man. We done been through shit together."

"I heard that. O.K., here it is. Some big wigs in D.C. want me to kill the end of the 'ghetto crisis' series. They don't want to hear anything about 'ghetto blaster'."

Dap looked genuinely puzzled.

"What the fuck do they care? If you write about it or if you don't write about it, motherfuckers gon' still be doin' it."

"I know...and that's what makes it even stronger. My editor thinks that some upper snot bureaucrat may have his fingers in the pie some kind of way. We don't quite know where to put things. It's a real puzzler. The other thing is this: I copped a couple grams of 'ghetto blaster'."

Dap Sugar bristled at his friend, his teeth showing.

"Don't touch that shit, Cran...if you want some coke, c'mon 'n see me. I can get you some pure Bolivian. I don't know what they 'stompin' that 'blaster' with."

"I didn't make a buy for my personal use, I bought some and had it analyzed at a friend's private pharmaceutical lab. The shit ain't cocaine, Dap."

"What?!"

"I said—the shit ain't real cocaine. It tests out to be cocaine in almost every way, but it's not."

He watched Dap's head tilt up to look in the ceiling, "April in Paris" drifting from the back speaker.

"According to my friend, someone has created a synthetic product that's ninety-nine percent like the real thing and fifty percent more addictive."

"Oh wowww!"

"He took me through a mountain of chemistry, trying to

explain shit. The bottom line is that some fuckin' genius has developed a fake cocaine and has dumped it in the ghettos. The shit is so complex he couldn't do anything but explain that it was fake, but he didn't know how to duplicate it."

Roger watched Dap lean forward to rest his head on the steering wheel. He looked despondent.

"Roger, you know me, man, we been tight a long time."

He lifted his head from the wheel...

"And I think you know that I be doin' my share of dirt, just like everybody else. I'm sure you know that, don't you?"

Roger nodded in agreement.

"But I never took to lyin', I hate a liar worse than God hates little green apples. I'd rather have a motherfucker steal from me than lie to me. Now what I'm gonna say to you is God's truth...number one, I didn't know the shit wasn't real. Number two, I didn't want to fuck with it personally because I didn't like what it did to a chump."

"But you were willing to sell it?"

"Roger, you can't cop an attitude. If I wasn't selling it somebody else would be doin' it. It's just plain 'n simple business."

"And you have no idea where it comes from?"

"I'm gonna make it my business to find out."

He pushed his hand out for the soul shake.

"Rog, you know I've sometimes given you tips 'n shit that operated against my own interests in a way, but if I could see the validity of what you were doin'...above 'n beyond my bullshit, I'd go on and thaw you out. You know that?"

"I know, Dap, I know. Hey, give my regards to your lady, she's a beautiful sister. I'm gonna try to get home to mine before midnight."

"You late already, Cran, you late already!"

***

143

Colonel Malan sat across from "Mr. Smith" in the Sun City Cafe, sipping a tall lemonade. "Mr. Smith" nursed a glass of scotch and soda.

They had felt it best to meet outside of any of the major population centers in South Africa.

"I appreciate you taking the time to meet with me, Mr. Smith."

"Well, as you know, I have been a part of the negotiating team in Angola, a secret part, but a part nevertheless."

They exchanged coded spy-smiles.

"Now then, what I have to say to you regarding 'Operation Cobra' may not be pleasant but I trust you will understand that I am speaking on behalf of a higher authority."

"I quite understand, Mr. Smith."

He shuffled his back in the cushioned chair. The stitches were still irritating him. ANC bastards . . .

"We feel that your 'activities' have been totally successful up to a point. I'm sure you'll agree that your visual disinformation campaign has been successful."

Malan nodded pleasantly. What's the point, "Mr. Smith?"

"But now we're beginning to experience serious problems, as a result of aiding, or at least abetting you with your campaign.

"There is an extremely strong anti-drug lobby pushing for stronger penalties against pushers and that sort of thing. When we can't seem to control this problem, it offers the American voter a jaundiced look at his government. I think you'll agree that we've been most cooperative."

Malan gave another pleasant nod.

"We've even gone so far as to try to put a lid on information that might damage your p.r. efforts, but now, with the arrest of one of your people and the suicide of another one, the woman, we're going to have to ask you to cease and desist.''

It was time to play hardball.

"And what if we are not ready to 'cease and desist' at this time?"

"I can hardly imagine that you would want to have unbearable pressures brought to bear on your operation."

"I'm certain that the people who aided us in the development of this operation, or at least abetted us, would hardly be in a position to bring unbearable pressures to bear."

"By many other names, that sounds like the terms for a blackmail."

"I don't mean to make it sound that way."

"Mr. Smith" drained his glass and matched "Iceberg" Malan's hard look.

"Look, Colonel, the jig is up. We've stroked your back and you've stroked ours, now it's time for us to quit stroking each other for awhile. We do not want to get caught with our thumbs stuck in our asses, hoping that a sympathetic white public will forgive us for helping the apartheid regime string the inner city out."

"String the inner city out?"

"Create a serious drug problem in the ghettos."

"I'll have to consult my . . ."

"Consult whomever you like, but have your operation dismantled within the next month or face the consequences. Afternoon, sir."

The two men stood and shook hands, appearing to the casual observer like two businessmen concluding a successful deal.

Colonel Malan settled back to think for a minute. Was "Mr. Smith" simply threatening him to get a reaction, or was the situation serious?

It didn't help matters to have Hans Botha in jail and Anna Viloen dead. They could have at least had the decency to complete their missions before going off the deep end.

"Another lemonade, suh?"

He frowned at the smiling Black face.

"No, thank you."

***

Jimmy Morgan, export/import, Anna Viloen, South African jewelry store owner. The two figures kept popping through his consciousness.

He decided to satisfy his curiosity.

"Jackie Jenkins, I have a little piece of business I want you to help me with."

"I'd be more than happy to help you with any little piece you want."

She was disappointed that he only wanted to use her charming telephone personality, but cooperated anyway.

After two days, they were able to locate Mr. Jimmy Morgan. He had coached Jackie Jenkins thoroughly and sat on the other side of the desk, writing questions for her and taking notes. A woman's voice would work miracles, at times.

"Yes, Mr. Morgan, my name is Freda Soza and I received this letter from my friend Anna only two days before...before her death."

Skip the theatrics, Jackie, just stay with the script.

"She knew I was coming and she spoke about you in her letters."

"Are you an Afrikaner, too?" he asked suddenly.

"No, I am not. I am a Pondo, an African."

Good play, Jackie, good play.

"You're Black, and you say Anna was a friend of yours?"

"I don't quite understand, Mr. Morgan."

"Never mind. What is it you wanted?"

146

"Well, I'll be coming to Chicago next...next month and I wanted to talk with you about her, to get a chance to find out what happened from someone who loved her."

"I didn't love her and if you knew what I knew, you couldn't possibly think of her as a friend. Goodbye, Ms. Soza."

They sat for a pregnant moment, looking around.

"You say this guy was this woman's lover?"

"That's what the paper said."

"'If you knew what I knew'—what's that supposed to mean?"

"Jackie, luv, your guess is absolutely as good as mine. You were fantastic. That little hint of a Jamaican patois is what did it."

"Little hint of patois?! Mon, I'll have you know that my folks come from Barbados, not Jamaica anything!"

"Jackie, you are full of surprises."

"How would you know," she asked, and strutted back to the Ads department.

If you knew what I knew...

If you knew what I knew...

Oh, well, I've had my little kick for the day, time to get back to the drawing board.

***

Dap Sugar stood in front of John Van Niekerk, fashionably decked out in a black velvet jogging suit, black chamois gloves on, a black leather cap pulled to the left side of his head.

He plastered another strip of adhesive across Van Niekerk's mouth, tested the clothesline he had tied him into his office chair with, his hands strapped to the arm rests.

He leaned over to wipe sweat from Van Niekerk's brow

and proceeded to lay his "tools" on the desk in front of Van Niekerk's frightened eyes. An old-fashioned straight razor, an ice pick, a pair of pliers, a hypodermic needle. He pocketed the Walter P.38 that had made Van Niekerk his captive.

"O.K., Van Neekick, we're gonna find out what you know. I gave you a chance to answer a couple simple questions and you come off with this cutie-pie shit. I told you when I came in here that I wanted answers to questions and I'm gonna get answers to questions or else you gon' have a hard time gettin' up in the mornin'."

He turned to make certain that the "closed" sign was in the gallery window, that the answering machine was on. It would never to do have someone call and not receive an answer.

"Now here's how we gonna do this. I'm gonna put this ballpoint in your hand. Uh huh, kinda hard to hold with your hand tied up like that, but don't worry, we can loosen it a bit at the proper time. I also have a li'l pad for you to write on. O.K., we all set?"

He smiled maliciously.

"All you gotta do is signal that you wanna write when I ask you a question. Got it?"

Van Niekerk used his eyes to convey his contempt.

"Uh huh, just as I thought, one o' them arrogant motherfuckers."

Dap Sugar Charlie, a Vietnam vet who had participated in a half dozen "interrogation" sessions conducted by Korean marines, picked up the pliers and deftly pulled Van Niekerk's left thumbnail out. Van Niekerk's eyes walled back and his whole body recoiled from the pain.

"What I found out in Vietnam is that if you gon' make a motherfucker spill his guts, then you got to get right to the point."

He spoke quietly, like a dentist filling a cavity. He placed the pliers, still clenching the thumbnail, on the desk.

"O.K., now then, how about a little razor work? But first we need something to..."

He strolled to the toilet, leaving Van Niekerk to stare at his thumbnail. He returned with a roll of toilet paper.

"Now then..."

He neatly, surgically severed the second joint of the middle finger on Van Niekerk's left hand and immediately wrapped layers of toilet paper around it to staunch the flow of blood.

He gently placed the finger beside the thumbnail.

"You wanna answer my questions now?"

Van Niekerk, trembling, white-faced, signaled "Yes."

"Now you actin' like a sensible white boy."

Dap loosened the rope strapping his right hand to the arm rest and placed a pad for him to write on.

Van Niekerk wrote, "Fuck you, nigger."

Dap looked at the scrawled words and smiled viciously.

"Uhh ohh, one o' them, huh? Well, ain't no sense tryin' to be nice to you. I was gonna give your ass a break but you one o' them Nazi motherfuckers, huh?"

Dap picked up the hypodermic needle.

"You know what we got in here, buddy? We got enough contaminated blood to kill your ass ten times. How about it?"

He tore Van Niekerk's sleeve off and held the needle up, looking for a vein. Van Niekerk squirmed frantically, indicating he would talk.

He held the pad in place, the needle still poised.

"Question, where does 'ghetto blaster' come from? Who makes it?"

Van Niekerk, his eyes wobbling from pain and fear, scribbled, "South Africa."

Dap stared at the words, and snatched the tape from Van Niekerk's mouth.

149

"If you make one loud sound, I'll push this needle right in your fuckin' eye. You understand?"

Van Niekerk stared down at his thumbnail and his finger and nodded yes, he understood.

"What's South Africa mean?"

It came out in a gush, the spare-my-life confession.

Dap Sugar sat back on the desk, almost sitting on Van Niekerk's finger at the conclusion.

"Well, I'll be goddamned! You mean you tellin' me the absolute God in Heaven truth?!"

"Yes, yes, I swear," Van Niekerk was blubbering. He couldn't take his eyes off the needle in Dap's hand.

"Now, once again, gimme these names. No, write the motherfuckers down. I'll never be able to remember all these foreign names."

Van Niekerk wrote —Hans Botha, Claus Van Der Merwe, Anna Viloen, Colonel Henrik Malan.

"These are the rotten motherfuckers who was bringing the shit in, huh? Including you. And y'all be usin' ignunt ass niggers like me to get the shit down into the 'hood, huh?"

Van Niekerk nodded numbly.

Dap slapped a fresh swatch of tape across Van Niekerk's mouth and held the needle up to the light and pushed its contents out.

"I didn't have nothin' in here but some red-colored water, Kneecrunch, nothin' but colored water. But I don't blame you, if somebody had threatened my life with AIDS, I'd give it up too."

He reassembled his "tools," removing Van Niekerk's thumbnail from the grip of the pliers.

"Here, you keep this, and this ol' piece o' finger too."

He rolled the "tools" up and placed them in a small black toolbox, except for his ice pick.

"If you hadn't called me a nigger, Kneecrunch, I might've

would've let you live, but you called me a nigger 'n I don't like that.''

He methodically plunged the ice pick into Van Niekerk's right ear, both eyes, his heart, and walked behind the chair to give him the coup d' grace.

On his way out, he paused in front of ''The Washer Woman'' and ripped a giant X from one side of the painting to another.

Chapter 12

Crystal Cranberry frowned at the phone ringing.

Damn! Two O'clock.

"Yawwwwn...yes?"

"Sorry to wake you up, Crystal, but I gotta talk to Roger, this is Dap."

"I know...yawwwnnn...I recognize your voice. Can't it wait 'til tomorrow morning, he just dozed off?"

"I'm awake, who is it?"

"Dap Sugar."

"Roger, I just found out some hellified shit, man, I don't wanna talk about it on the phone."

"That important, huh?"

"That important."

"Well, c'mon then."

"See you in a minute."

Crystal made coffee and tried to ignore the specs of blood

on Dap's jogging suit. In an uncharacteristically quiet voice, he gave them the story Van Niekerk had given him.

"Oh, here are their names."

Roger spilled his coffee.

"Botha, the Aryan Circle Nazi, Anna Viloen! These are the coordinators, were the coordinators?!"

"He wasn't lyin', man, I put him in a position not to lie, believe me..."

Cranberry stared at the names, his mind blistering events and circumstances together. What the hell was going on here?

"And you're saying that they were doing all of this to take them off of TV?!"

"Just goes to show you how important the boob-tube is."

The three of them sipped their coffee for a few beats.

"Dap, I don't really know what to say to you, man, you know what this means?"

"Don't say shit, Cran; I mean, you know what I mean? I may be a fuckin' thug but I'm still a Black thug. Can you dig where I'm comin' from?"

They shook hands. Crystal circled the table and planted a passionate kiss on his left cheek.

***

Roger Cranberry strode briskly into the office, feeling alert, positive, despite the fact that he had only three hours sleep. He made a wide detour to whisper into Jackie Jenkins' ear, "Morning, beautiful."

She reacted by mistyping half a sentence.

He sat at his desk, breathing hard, trying to collect his thoughts. This was the "ghetto crisis" story of all stories.

His desk phone ringing startled him. He stirred himself, notes in hand, to the editor's office. Wait until he hears this...

"Roger, sit down. We got not good news and not bad news, but odd news. The big boys have backed off. They no longer think that the 'ghetto crisis' series will threaten national security."

Roger Cranberry rehearsed a Dap Sugar level laugh and then explained to his editor what the real deal was.

"Well, I'll be damned."

"And we got documented evidence."

"No one will believe it, Roger, you know that, don't you?"

"Sam, with a story like this, I'm willing to become the Jesse Jackson of journalism, I can't lose even if I lose."

"Morgan is the linchpin, huh?"

"Not completely, but he is important."

"When're you leaving?"

"This evening, if possible."

"Noreen, we want a seat on the evening flight to Chicago, round trip, open end, for Roger Cranberry."

"Thanks, Sam."

"Get outta here, Roger."

"Oh, when do you want to spring this out?"

"You'll be back on Monday, let's look at a finished product on Wednesday."

"Sounds right."

On the plane, Roger stared at the article on page three as though he were hypnotized. "Hans Botha, stabbed to death in prison."

Crystal's advice wedged back up into his consciousness. "Be careful of those motherfuckers, Roger, they're treacherous."

Chicago. Chicago was a lakefront, concerts in the park, midnight jazz sets, blues on the westside. He had never had anything to do with a Jimmy Morgan, a brother who lived on the northside, in Chicago.

Morgan met him at the door with one word, "Cranberry?" and led him into a room that looked like a medieval dining hall.

"Make yourself at home. Drink?"

He nodded yes, a bit awed by his surroundings.

"Cognac?"

"That would be fine."

So, this is what third generation Black money looked like.

He handed him a snifter of cognac and settled into the sofa that faced an enormous fireplace.

"Please, sit down."

He waited for Roger Cranberry to take a sip of his cognac before speaking.

"You want to know something about my relationship to Anna, what do you want to know?"

A no-nonsense type, good. The sooner he got what he needed, the better.

"Well, why don't we start at the beginning? That would be a good place to start from."

Jimmy Morgan started from the beginning, hesitated a bit in the middle and cried a little at the ending.

"Can you imagine what it would feel like, falling in love with a woman like that?"

Roger, on his third cognac, found it difficult to imagine.

"And she gave no indication, before the end, that she was...well, what she was?"

"No, no hint at all. Incidentally, your secretary, or whatever she is, deserves a raise..."

They exchanged smug smiles.

"I have to ask you this, what do you think made her surrender, give up her cover?"

Jimmy Morgan, poor li'l rich Black man, looked around at his enviornment for a few seconds.

"Well, I'm not an unattractive man. I really think it was

155

me, the possibility of us getting together. I think that's what made her come to her senses."

There, the essential stuff was settled in place. Now for the spice, the color.

"Mr. Morgan, do you think you were targeted?"

"Targeted?"

"Well, you know, picked out as a figure to be developed in Anna Viloen's scheme of things?"

"Naw, like I told you, I hit on her."

"Are you certain?"

"Mr. Cranberry, take my word for it, I know what seduction looks like."

The interview wound down to a polite ending.

"It looks like we covered the whole thing."

"I want to thank you for giving me the opportunity to tell my side of this thing. I wasn't looking forward to telling my children one day, or trying to tell my children, that I wasn't involved with an Afrikaner who was trying to poison our people."

They shook hands, warmly. Poor brother, Roger thought, strolling to his rent-a-car. Poor brother, to have Anna Viloen in your memory.

He sprawled across the bed in his hotel room, staring up at the ceiling, trying to figure out a way to write about the whole thing. Truth is stranger than fiction.

***

"I don't think you should feel that we lost the war, Henrik, it was only one battle."

"Yessir, I understand that."

I understand that it was all in vain, that the country is being blown apart by terrorists, that we are surrendering to the Blacks. I understand that my cleverly orchestrated attempt

156

to put our best face forward has been withdrawn, for political reasons.

"I realize that it may seem like a terrific battle has been lost, on the surface, but in reality, it hasn't. We are not the losers, they are. We are withdrawing from the trenches, having lost only four, but they have lost thousands. I consider that victory, don't you, Henrik?"

It was impossible to argue with the old man's logic. But was he so blinded by his own rhetoric that he couldn't see the handwriting on the wall?

Kattenbrunner had been assasinated in the Transkei by an unknown party or parties. Neither the ANC nor any of the extremist groups had claimed credit for the murder. And the formula for "ghetto blaster" had been buried with him.

We should have interrogated him to get the formula. It would have been an excellent weapon to use in our own Bantustans.

Bombs were going off night and day and people were deserting the ship. Rats. The ones who could afford it were going to Europe, America, South America.

The Blacks were coming into power, there was no doubt about it, and he hated the idea.

"I guess that's all we have to deal with for the moment, Henrik. If there's anything else, you know how to reach me."

"Yessir."

The president opened the door, paused.

"Incidentally, how's Greta, Henrik?"

He thought he detected the hint of a humorous gleam in the old man's eyes.

"Oh, she's fine, sir, just fine."

"Good, I like the idea of good marriages amongst my people, it creates worthwhile images for the younger folks and, as you know, one good image is worth a thousand words. 'Night, Henrik?''

Malan sat at the table, his hands folded in front of him. It was coming to an end, he could sense it with every nerve in his body. Black policemen were completely untrustworthy, if they could be found at all. The few multinational forms still operating in this country were like hens sitting on eggs, waiting to see what would hatch.

The unspeakable was happening. South Africa was becoming something called Azania.

***

Roger Cranberry literally floated through, on his way to Sam Walters' office. Was he going to receive a raise? A syndicated column? A two-week vacation in the Bahamas?

"You wanted to see me, Sam?"

"Yeah, pull up a chair, let's go over your piece."

Roger sat, crossed his legs, exuded confidence.

"To begin with, I'd like to say that the piece is extremely well written. You've dotted all your i's and crossed all of your t's. Extremely well done."

"Thanks, Sam."

"There's just one problem, Roger; we can't print it."

"What?!"

Cranberry popped from the chair as though he had sat on a tack. Sam Walters placed both palms out at him, a calming gesture.

"Let me explain, Roger, please. Just let me explain, okay?"

Cranberry perched on the edge of the chair, angry and hurt.

"Man, do you know how much effort I put into that piece?!"

"I know you put a lot into it, Roger, it shows. Just gimme a few minutes to explain why we can't deal with it in the

Vista. Number one, we've had the rug pulled from under us by the big-wigs. If we printed your story just as you've written it, we'd be the laughing stock of the newspaper business."

Roger sat, bristling.

"Go on, I'm listening."

"What's happened is that you've uncovered a rat-cheese relationship that the biggies don't want exposed. And they're prepard to go to any lengths to prevent that exposure.

"'Mr. Smith' called again last night, we had a very lengthy chat. He made me clearly understand what the consequences could be for printing the 'inventions' of an overly-imaginative writer."

"But it's all there; the people, the connections, everything!"

"I'm totally aware of that, but like I said, they've pulled the rug from under us. They're prepared to issue denials, from the highest level, that anything like an Afrikaner conspiracy was ever allowed to function in this country."

"But Sam, the people...?"

"Roger, bear with me, the people are gone. Botha was stabbed to death in prison, Viloen committed hari-kari, Van Neikerk was tortured and killed by the Mafia, at least that's what the story is."

"We still have Van Der Merwe."

"Claus Van Der Merwe was denied political asylum and shipped back to South Africa yesterday, under close guard."

"Well, I'll be damned! That was kinda sudden, wasn't it?"

"That's what I said, too."

Roger gestured wildly, "Morgan! Morgan! The Black guy in Chicago who was Viloen's lover?"

Sam Walters held out a clipping from a Chicago area newspaper.

"James Morgan, wealthy Black entrepreneur—killed by

159

burglers in early morning burglary."

"The bastards think of everything, don't they?"

Walters noddd in agreement.

"Roger, I know how you feel, believe me. I was a bang-tailed reporter too, once upon a time. Nothing hurts worse than having a story squashed."

"It's not so much the story, Sam, it's what's behind the story. Do you have any idea how many addicts these motherfuckers left behind?! I can't just simply look at that and write it off as a story that was nipped."

"Roger, like I said, I understand how you feel, but what can we do? If we defy the would-be censors and publish the story, how in the hell could we back it up? What kind of proof could we offer to substantiate these allegations? I've been wracking my brain to come up with something, and so far zero!

"I want to publish this piece as badly as anything we've published, but we have the paper's reputation to consider."

Cranberry stood up, looking down at Walters' desk, shaking his head.

"I just can't let it go, Sam. I just can't drop it like that."

"Roger, why don't you take a couple days off? Give it some thought. If you can come in with a concrete angle, we'll go to work on 'em. Okay?"

"Yeah, sure Sam."

He shuffled back to his desk to call his wife.

"Roger, how did it go, when will it be out?"

"It didn't go, it won't be out."

"What did you say?"

"I'll tell you about it when you get home."

He sat at his desk looking so disgusted, Ms. Jackie Jenkins tip-toed past and decided not to ask him what he thought of her new blouse.

***

"Roger, check this out. This is the sixth, no, the eighth one this week. Known drug dealer found in Dempsey dumpster, ice-picked to death. A copied note was found stuffed in his mouth—"Warning: Hard drug dealers will be given one warning. If they persist in their activities, they will be executed."

"Looks like somebody has gotten kinda serious, huh?"

"Looks that way. I just hate that it has to go to the vigilante level."

"Yeah, that gets to me, too. But what can you do once things get to a certain point?"

They sat in the breakfast nook, enjoying a late Saturday morning, exchanging sections of the Los Angeles Vista, thumbing through their mail.

"Baby, did you see this? We got a card from Dap."

"Dap? Where is he?"

"The card is from Angola..."

"Angola?!"

"That's what it says, 'Welcome to Angola', but it's postmarked from Libya."

"Looks like the brother is doin' a li'l travelin'."

They exchanged eye signals and made no other comments about Dap Sugar Charlie.

"Crystal, I've reached a decision about that piece. I'm going to expand it and make a novel out of it. It'll be fictional, of course, because none of the facts are true. Right? Let's see what they do about that."

She walked around to his side of the table and sat in his lap.

"I just love your mind, do you know that?"

"That all?"

She responded with a deep kiss.

"Hmmmmmmm..."

***

161

Colonel Malan stared down at the cold blue waters of the south Atlantic Ocean and gritted his teeth. He had read the handwriting on the wall and decided to take an extended "vacation." The president had encouraged him.

"It will make things a little easier, politically, you understand what I mean, Henrik?"

Karl Strausser had opened the doors of his home to him.

"Yes, of course you may come, Henrik. You may stay as long as you like."

"Thank you, Herr Strausser, I deeply appreciate your offer. I can assure you that we are doing all we can to apprehend the person, or persons, responsible for Dr. Kattenbrunner's murder."

"Ah, yes, of course, Colonel Malan. He was such a young man and had so much scientific knowledge."

He felt like crying but braced himself against the idea. What the hell was there to cry about? The battle was still being fought but the war was over. Any fool could see that.

They were six months away from Mandela's release and when that happened, he felt certain, Pretoria would become an isolated white enclave. The Blacks, eighty-seven percent of the population, now occupying thirteen percent of the land, were going to reverse the situation in short order. They had every reason to want to do so.

He didn't see his "vacation" in Argentina as a permanent situation, rather, a way to get out of the fire for a moment, to regroup. South Africa would never revert to the "uncivilized" place his ancestors had found.

The Americans would finance contra-type insurgencies, he felt certain of that. They were not going to start dealing with the natives about the diamonds, gold, uranium and other minerals so long as there was one white man is position to be dealt with.

"Henrik?"

He turned from staring at the ocean to look into his wife's watery blue eyes.

"Yes, Greta, what is it?"

"I want to thank you for...for...taking me with you."

"I had no choice. Don't thank me."

He ignored her soft sobs, absorbed by the thoughts of what had to be done to regain the upper hand in his country.

***

"Crystal, what in the world are you doing?"

"I'm packing. What's it look like I'm doing?"

"You going somewhere?"

"We're going somewhere."

"Oh. Any place in particular?"

"In three months or so, we'll be trying to get visas 'n stuff to go to Angola."

"Angola?!"

"Man, you sound like a parrot. Yes, Angola. We don't want to fly into Azania, we want to walk in, right?"

He grabbed her around the waist and swung her around gently.

"I love you, you know that?"

"I think that's a nice prerequisite for this baby we're planning to have, don't you?"

"I totally agree. Well, I guess I better start packing, too. It never hurts to be prepared, Dap says..."

"Dap Sugar Charlie?"

"Yeah. He got through to me at the office today. He was calling from Paris."

"Hahhh hahh...that dude is something else. What did he have to say?"

"He asked me to let him know when we planned to trip

to Angola, he'll send Shebelle down to open up his house for us, Shebelle and this other woman that he's married to. He says her name sounds like Okrah, or Oprah or something like that."

"That brother is too much, too much..."

"Baby, did we drink all of the Beaujolais Villages?"

Post-Script

Nelson Mandela was finally released (February 11, 1990) from prison after serving more than twenty-seven years. The latest designer drug, popularly known as "ice," has also been released. The effect of "ice" is known to be fifty times as strong and lasts one hundred times longer than "crack." Which government is responsible for its distribution? Where will it surface next?

The beat goes on.

Epilogue

O.K., I read it three times (Muntuna read half of it and gave up—"It's too weird for my taste") and each time I read it I seemed to be climbing onto another layer.

After I finished it the last time, we pulled the Chivas Regal back out from its hiding place and rapped.

"Leon, bottom line, all I can say to you, brother, is that you sure in fuck make it seem like it could've been true."

He stared into my eyes for a hard minute before replying.

"That's all I wanted to do, man, that's all I wanted to do: make it seem like the shit could've been real."